DREAMS CHANGE

A River Dream Novel

DW Davis

River Sailor Literary

River Sailor
Literary

eBook ISBN: 9780983355625
Paperback ISBN: 9780983355632
Hardcover ISBN: 979831265676

Cover design by Ashley Bratcher
Cover Image (c) Lydia Sanchez
https://www.flickr.com/photos/93963757@N05/

*This book is dedicated to the sailing staff at Camp
Don Lee who encouraged my love of sailing.*

CONTENTS

CHAPTER ONE

The Neuse River doesn't roll between New Bern and Oriental; it rises and falls with the tide.

Summer was nearly over. The evening breeze brought the promise of cooler fall days to come. Dusk fell on the river, turning the water gray and gradually hiding the far shore in darkness.

Far shore was an apt description. On that part of the river, the south shore was over four miles away. Sitting alone at the end of the dock at River Dream, drinking a nice cold glass of iced tea, I was thinking about all that had happened to me in the four years since high school graduation.

My years in the Navy were exciting, exhausting, exhilarating, and ultimately excruciating. Training was tough, but the missions were tougher. Nothing we did ever made the papers. It wasn't supposed to.

I'd joined to put in my four years before going

home to marry Rhiannon and start college. Little did I know how drastically those plans would change when we shipped out on what would become my last mission. It was a mission I almost didn't make it back from. It took the Navy doctors a while to fix me up.

By the time the Navy decided to give me a medical discharge, I could walk without crutches, or even a cane. In fact, I barely showed a limp and felt ready to return to duty.

The Navy felt differently. It didn't need someone with a replacement hip and titanium screws holding his leg together. On the day I walked out of Bethesda, my mom and dad were there. Rhiannon wasn't. I guess she'd decided she didn't need me anymore either.

After more than a year of enduring seemingly endless rounds of surgery and excruciating sessions of physical therapy, I'd finally accepted the fact that Rhiannon wasn't going to come. She hadn't come to see me at the hospital. She hadn't come while I was going through those months of rehabilitation. She hadn't come at all. As each day went by that she didn't show up, my hopes dimmed and my love for her grew colder.

Rhiannon was working in Africa for the Peace Corps when I got wounded. She'd taken a break from Dartmouth for that. My folks contacted the Peace Corps to get word to her. Rhiannon sent back word to keep her informed about how I was doing. She wrote she hoped I'd be up and about soon.

My mother tried to communicate to her about the

seriousness of my situation. I wrote and asked her to come home to be with me. Rhiannon replied she couldn't just up and leave her work. She never came.

I spent forever in that hospital as they put my hip and leg back together and taught me how to walk again. The day after forever, I went home to River Dream. I took out our prom picture and felt nothing but bitter regret. I threw the picture away.

I returned to North Carolina and River Dream on June 9, 1983, four years to the day after I'd graduated from Laney High School. I spent the summer in introspection and reflection, combined with a lot of sailing.

Sailing was my solace that summer. Maybe I was of no use to the Navy, but I could still sail. Summer passed slowly as time on the river healed my spirit and my body. Before I knew it, the time arrived for freshman orientation at the University of North Carolina at Wilmington. I got settled into my dorm, met my roommate, bought my books, and prepared to begin my higher education. It was a chance to start over. I intended to make the most of it.

CHAPTER TWO

August 1983

Sitting in my dorm room unpacking, I noticed a dark-skinned young man standing in the door looking at me with a puzzled expression on his face. He was wearing a Manteo High Redskins T-shirt, a pair of well-worn blue jeans, and a pair of Topsider boat shoes without socks. That spoke well of him. Only nerds wore socks with Topsiders.

Without pausing in my unpacking, I asked, "Can I help you?"

He tilted his head to one side, ran his free hand over his short-cropped black hair, and looked at the paper in his other hand.

"You Michael J. Lanier?"

I closed the drawer of my little dorm dresser, stood, and stretched.

"That's what it says on the checks the Navy sends me every month. And you are?"

"This here paper," he said, holding up the bright yellow piece of paper he'd gotten from the housing office, "says I'm your roommate. My name's Derrick, Derrick Carson."

I walked over to the door and held out my hand. Noticing I had a slight height advantage, I guessed Derrick stood just shy of six feet tall.

"Nice to meet you, Derrick. You can call me Mike."

Derrick hesitated before shaking my hand. His firm grip matched his athletic build.

"Dude, don't take this the wrong way or nothing, but ain't you kind of old for a freshman?"

Not that I was much older. I was only twenty-two at the time. To Derrick, those four years must have seemed like a generation.

"I did a hitch in the Navy after high school. Now I'm ready to get on with my higher education," I said in a lighthearted tone.

Derrick cracked a bit of a smile.

"Navy, huh? You from around here?"

"I grew up on Wrightsville Beach. My folks still live there."

Backing away from the door, I gestured for him to come on in. For the first time, a genuine smile appeared on his face.

"You're a beach bum, too. I grew up in Nags Head. Graduated from Manteo High last June."

Learning I was a fellow beach bum apparently removed any doubts Derrick had about rooming with an old Navy vet like me.

CHAPTER THREE

September 1983

Classes started out well. I found myself spending a lot of time in the Randall Library studying and doing homework. The dorms were great places for socializing but lousy places for studying.

One night at the library, I spotted a familiar-looking girl with strawberry blond hair that fell in waves past her shoulders. Not sure it was really Maeve, I worked up the courage to walk over and say hello. That was as far as I got.

"Michael! Is that you? I thought my imagination might be playing tricks on me. What a surprise! What are you doing here?" Judging by Maeve's smile and the sparkle in her heather blue eyes, she was glad to see me.

"I'm from here, remember? I've been back in town since school started. I got out of the Navy in June and spent the summer up at my place near Camp

Riversail."

Maeve's eyes took on a faraway look. "I remember your place on the river." There was a hint of nostalgia in her voice. "But that's right; you actually lived at Wrightsville Beach."

Frowning, she tilted her head and said, "I never knew you were in the Navy."

Just as quickly, she was smiling again. "Are you going to school here now?"

Taking a seat, she gestured at the chair across the table from hers.

"What are you doing here at this time of night?"

I was having trouble keeping up with her. Accepting her unspoken offer to sit down, I replied, "I'm finishing up a paper that's due tomorrow. I usually work here in the library. The dorm's too full of distractions."

"Are you staying in the dorms?" Maeve seemed a bit surprised. "I figured you'd just commute from your place at the beach!"

"I don't actually live there anymore. My folks still do, but I wanted the full freshman experience. That meant living in the dorm. Now I wonder. I don't think I'll keep it up next semester."

"I think it's a good idea that you at least gave it a try." She snickered and said, "Bet you're a little older than most of the guys in your dorm. I stayed in the dorm my one glorious year at Yale. I did here, too, until last year. Now I've moved into an apartment off campus."

I smiled, remembering her telling me once she'd

rather go to the University of North Carolina than Yale. "You left Yale to come here?"

"I didn't like it up there. The winters were too long and cold, and the beaches just weren't real beaches, not in my book." She spread her hands symbolically taking in the whole school. "Besides, I can finish my degree here for what one more semester at Yale would have cost."

I nodded my understanding of that economic fact. "How much longer until you graduate?"

"This is my senior year," Maeve said as she pointed at the stack of books on the table. "And it's my busiest yet. That's what I get for taking a double major. We may see a lot of each other if you spend a lot of time in the library, because I'm here all the time. What you learned about the dorm I've found holds true in my apartment, too many distractions."

"Is your apartment close by?" It was meant to sound like a casual question, but Maeve picked up on the note of hopefulness I couldn't quite hide.

Maeve grinned, and her eyes brightened. "It's in University Apartments, right across College Road. It's so close I can walk to campus. Speaking of which, I suppose I should be walking home about now. I've got an early class tomorrow."

I noticed a flicker of regret in her eyes. Getting the feeling she was hoping I would, I said, "It's late. I'd feel better if I could see you safely home."

"Now that you mention it, if it wouldn't be out of your way, I wouldn't mind the company," Maeve said with a relieved smile.

I assured her it wasn't out of my way at all. If it had been 180 degrees out of my way, which in fact it was, I wouldn't have said so.

Maeve reached across the table and put her hand on mine. I noticed pale pink nail polish on her neatly trimmed nails. Then I felt a slight flutter in my chest when I saw that the only thing adorning her fingers was her high school ring.

"It's sure good to see you again, Michael. I've thought about you a lot since that summer."

My thoughts went back to the summer we spent together at Camp Riversail, and I smiled. My smile faded some when I thought of the day we'd said goodbye. Pushing that aside, I took her hands in mine. "I guess I should see you home."

Maeve checked to see that she hadn't left anything on the table. Then she looked up at me and smiled. "I'd like that."

Over the next couple of weeks, we developed a routine. Maeve and I would meet at the library in the evening, study together, and then I'd walk her home. The walks always ended with a polite good night at her front door.

Then, one Wednesday night, the routine changed. We left the library, and I walked her to her apartment as usual. All too soon we arrived at her door. I expected a polite thank you and a platonic parting. Maeve had something else in mind.

"Mike, would you like to come in? I could make some tea, or maybe a glass of wine."

Surprise must have shown clearly on my face as

she chuckled and then waited expectantly.

"Some tea would be nice." I'd never been much of a wine drinker.

"Okay, I'll make us some tea." She unlocked her door and led the way inside.

I asked about her roommate, and Maeve told me Kim - her roommate's name was Kim - was still at work. Kim's shift at the restaurant didn't get over until eleven, so she wouldn't be home until close to midnight. I still hadn't worked up the nerve to ask about Roger, or if there was someone else at all.

The apartment was small but tidy, decorated in contemporary American, with a living room, a kitchen with a compact dining area, two bedrooms, and a shared bath. The walls were all the same off-white color as my dorm room, and the carpeting was the same uniform light tan.

I sat in the only chair the living room boasted, an upholstered armchair with alternating dark and light brown stripes. Maeve went to the kitchen to heat water for tea. Responsibility for the décor rested squarely with Maeve's landlord. University Arms, which rented primarily to college students, provided only furnished apartments.

When Maeve came out of the kitchen, she sat on the end of the sofa closest to me. The sofa matched the pattern of the chair. In her usual bold manner, she came straight to the point.

"Mike, you haven't mentioned anything about a girlfriend. Are you seeing anyone?"

This was a sore point, but Maeve didn't know

that. "No. There was someone, but we aren't together anymore. I haven't seen her in quite a while." I couldn't hide the bitterness in my voice.

Maeve reached over and gripped my arm. "I'm sorry you broke up."

From the look on her face, she didn't seem too sorry. I decided not to correct her assumption that Rhiannon and I had broken up. We hadn't broken up. Rhiannon just never showed up, and eventually I accepted that.

The tea kettle started whistling. Maeve went to the kitchen and brought out steaming mugs.

"You need to let it steep for a few minutes to get the full flavor," she said as she handed me my cup. "I think you'll like it. It's one of my favorites."

She set her mug carefully on the coffee table and sat down. "So, have you found some nice college girl yet?"

I was hoping to find out if there was someone in her life first but decided to go out on a limb. "There is a special girl I knew several years ago. I ran into her again recently. I'm not sure how she feels about me, but I still have feelings for her."

Maeve was a very smart lady. I knew she knew I was talking about her, even though I didn't come right out and say so. This was the moment of truth. I waited to see how she'd react. She met my eyes and smiled sweetly.

"I think you'll find out she still has those feelings for you, too. She's felt that way about you for quite a while, you know."

My heart started racing in my chest. I couldn't believe what was happening. Maeve, the only girl who'd ever displaced Rhiannon in my heart, even if for just a short time one summer years before, was telling me she loved me, that she'd loved me ever since then. Realization, at once harsh and comforting, hit me. The future I'd imagined with Rhiannon was just an empty dream. Maybe Maeve was always supposed to be the one.

"Maeve, I hope she does because I know I do."

"Mike," Maeve said, her heather blue eyes glistening, "I do."

She set her teacup on the coffee table and leaned towards me. Setting my cup next to hers, I turned towards her, and we kissed. It was a gentle kiss; a long, gentle, tender kiss.

Then, her roommate came home. We turned towards the door as Kim came in. Her eyes widened as she noticed us.

"Oh, excuse me. It looks like I'm interrupting something."

"Um, well, to be quite honest, yes, you are," Maeve said, without a trace of embarrassment.

Shrugging her shoulders, Kim replied, "I'm as sorry as I can be, but I'm dead tired and just want to go to bed."

Feeling awkward now that her roommate was home, I decided it was time for me to leave. "I should probably get going anyway. I've got an early class."

"So do I," Maeve said.

About this time, we noticed Kim looking at us

with an impatient expression on her face.

"Well, is someone going to introduce me to this smokin' hot guy, or am I going to have to figure out who he is on my own?"

Maeve looked at me and tried to stifle a laugh. "Oh, sorry, yes. Kim Lee, meet Mike Lanier. Mike, this is my roommate Kim."

Kim was a beautiful second-generation Korean American. She had long black hair tied in a ponytail, dark brown eyes, and a slender build. She was wearing a light green golf shirt with the name of the restaurant where she worked embroidered on the left front, and a pair of tan chinos. As Maeve introduced us, a knowing look spread across Kim's face.

"Mike Lanier, *that* Mike." She smiled broadly and offered her hand. "It's nice to meet you, Mike Lanier."

"It's a pleasure to meet you, Kim."

I took Kim's extended hand and gave Maeve a puzzled glance.

"Yes, Kim, he's *that* Mike. Now, there's hot water on the stove for tea. Go fix yourself a cup while I say good night to Mike. Then we can talk."

"Okay, Maeve. See you later, Mike," Kim said before making her way to the kitchen.

"See you later, Kim," I said as I moved toward the door.

Maeve and I stepped out onto their small porch. Before I could ask, she explained. "You're probably wondering what Kim meant by 'that Mike,' right?"

Sensing she was a little nervous about having to explain, I teased her a bit by tilting my head to the side and biting my lip. "Now that you mention it, yes."

Maeve took a moment to decide how to say what she wanted to say. "You know how I said I'd felt *that way* about you for a while? Before, just before Kim came in."

She seemed very serious about what she was telling me, so I answered her seriously.

"I remember, yes."

"I trust Kim with anything, so I told her about you."

"When was this? I mean, how long -"

Maeve smiled, reached up, and gently touched my cheek. "The first night you walked me home from the library. And I told her about our summer together at camp. Back then, I thought we could never be together. When I saw you at the library the other night, I thought maybe now there's a chance."

I didn't know what to say. Since words failed me, I settled for action. I pulled Maeve to me and kissed her. It turned into a fairly passionate kiss for a front porch kiss. It took our breath away.

Stepping back, Maeve looked into my eyes and ran her fingers along my chin. "I should probably be getting back inside. I do have an early class tomorrow."

I reached up, took her hand, and kissed it. "Yes, I've got an eight o'clock class, too."

"Okay, then," Maeve said.

"Okay," I said.

We kissed again.

"Now, really, we need to say good night," Maeve

said, reaching for the door.

Reluctantly, I agreed. I stepped off the porch, turning back at the bottom step. Maeve blew me one more kiss before slipping through the door. My feet barely touched the ground as I headed back to my dorm.

My roommate, Derrick, was asleep when I got there. I quietly got ready for bed, but sleep wouldn't come. I replayed the evening over and over, afraid that if I fell asleep, I'd wake up and find out it was all a dream.

CHAPTER FOUR

September 1983

The alarm jolted me awake. If I didn't get moving, I'd be late for class. I hurried to the shower, rushed to get dressed, grabbed my books, and headed out the door. Realizing I'd forgotten my paper, I turned back. There on the desk, clipped to my assignment, was a note I hadn't seen before - a note with a phone number. Maeve must have clipped it to the paper when I visited the bathroom before leaving her apartment.

Here's my number just in case. See you at the library tonight.

Xoxo, Maeve

So, it wasn't a dream. I thought about calling her right then but realized two things. One, she was probably on her way to class, and two, I was about to be late for class. Having made it with a minute to spare, I turned in my paper and took my seat.

I barely noticed what the class was about, though I tried to concentrate and take notes. At the end of class, we were assigned another paper. That was all the class seemed to be about - writing papers. The Professor was cool, though. I supposed a scientist should know how to write papers. Besides, it gave me a reason to be in the library that night. Not that I needed one.

After English class, I had an hour before Statistics, so I headed over to the Seahawk's Nest, our student union, for some coffee and breakfast. They served a decent omelet, and the coffee wasn't bad.

Derrick was there when I got there. His first class on Thursday wasn't until eleven, the same time as my Statistics class. He got up early every morning and headed to the gym.

Derrick was big into martial arts. Sometimes we worked out together in the afternoon. I'd earned my black belt by high school, and the Navy taught me some interesting things about hand-to-hand fighting. Still, with my hip, I wasn't as quick as I needed to be, and Derrick usually beat me.

"Hey, Mike, how's it goin'?" Derrick asked around a mouthful of sausage biscuit.

I set my coffee down and slid into the seat across from him. "It's going pretty good. How 'bout you?"

He gulped some orange juice to wash down his biscuit. "I'm doing okay. Man, what time did you get back last night? I didn't hear you come in."

Since the Nest didn't have real maple syrup for me to sweeten my coffee with, I stirred in a spoonful of sugar. "Close to midnight. I came in playing a tuba and beating a drum. You didn't hear that?"

"Nah, man, you know I can sleep through

anything. Really though, what kept you out so late? That's not like you."

He was right. I was usually an early-to-bed, early-to-rise kind of guy. Thinking he'd be surprised to learn why I'd been late, I tried to sound nonchalant. "I was spending time with a lady friend."

Derrick swallowed the last bite of his biscuit and nodded his head. "No doubt. Anybody I know?"

"I don't think so. We spent a summer together at camp, back when I was in high school."

Derrick's eyes widened at the way the thought of that summer made me smile.

"I ran into her a couple of weeks ago at the library. I've walked her home each night since. Last night she invited me in."

I tried making it sound like no big deal.

"Man, that's cool," Derrick said before draining the last of his orange juice. "You guys gonna start dating? I hope so. You need something to take your mind off the books now and then."

I was thinking the same thing. "We'll have to wait and see how it goes. Right now, it looks promising."

Derrick nodded as he picked up his books and rose to leave. "Cool, man. Look, I got to run. Later."

Finished with breakfast, I spent some time going over my Statistics homework. I didn't like Statistics much, but it was required for my degree program. I muddled through class and then was done for the day.

After lunch, I met Derrick at the gym. He tried to beat me to a pulp, but in a friendly way. Derrick kept telling me I was getting better. I only spent half as much time on the mat as I did when we started working out together.

His saying so made me feel better, but not much. I headed back to the dorm for a shower and a change of clothes before going to the library.

When I got to the room, our phone was ringing. For an exorbitant fee, we'd had a phone installed in our dorm room. For an additional fee, we also got a small refrigerator. I was willing to pay the fees, and Derrick insisted on paying half.

I couldn't imagine who'd be calling, except maybe Derrick's folks, or mine. Figuring I'd better answer in either case, I picked up the phone and said, "Hello."

It was neither. "Hi, Mike, it's Maeve."

"Yes, it is. I mean, Hi, Maeve." I grimaced at how that must have sounded.

"Surprised?"

"Yeah. I didn't know you knew this number. I should have given it to you, but -"

"I took a chance and called the campus directory service. Sure enough, you were listed. So, I thought I'd call. I have an idea. You're going to the library tonight, right?"

"I'm on my way over there in just a few minutes. Hopefully, I can get my Biology done before supper, since I have another English paper to work on tonight."

"Supper is what I want to talk to you about. I was almost thinking you could come over, and we could get a pizza or something, before heading to Randall."

"That would be super, having supper together at

your place." I cringed and thought to myself, smooth Mike, real smooth. "What time should I come over?"

"I just got off work and need to change." Maeve had a work-study job at the campus bookstore in the afternoon. She needed the job, thanks to the chunk her one glorious year at Yale took out of her college fund.

"You could bring your work and do it here, couldn't you? I mean, while we wait for the pizza? That way you could get some done before we go to the library."

"Sure, I could do that. I just need to grab a quick shower. Derrick and I just got done working out at the gym."

"Derrick?" Maeve asked.

I could tell from her tone she was trying to place the name. "My roommate. Maybe we should introduce him to Kim. I suppose she might think he's a 'smokin' hot guy'."

"Oh, I remember you telling me about him." She chuckled as she caught my reference to Kim's comment. "Kim has a boyfriend. I'll order the pizza. You hurry up and get over here."

I responded with military precision. "Yes, ma'am, right away, ma'am."

Maeve laughed. "You brat, see ya soon."

I hurried through my shower and was at her door in a very short while. I drove. Hearing me pull up outside, she was waiting at the door, wearing a dark blue Yale Bulldogs T-shirt and a white tennis skirt that showed off her shapely legs. Catching sight of my GTO, her eyes widened. "Nice car."

Resting my hand protectively on the ragtop, I grinned like a proud papa. "Thanks. I almost sold the old Goat when I joined the Navy. My father talked me into keeping it."

As I walked through the door, Maeve put her arms around me and kissed me.

My eyes widened in surprise. "Wow, let me go back out and come in again."

Maeve smiled and pulled me back. "No need to do that." She kissed me again thoroughly.

"Do you wanna know what I was thinking about all day?" Maeve asked as we moved into the living room.

I sat on the couch and took a wild guess. "How much you love school?"

She smacked me lightly on the shoulder as she sat down beside me. "Brat! I was thinking about how much I was looking forward to seeing you tonight."

I pulled her to me and kissed her, not quite gently, but quite passionately.

Pausing to catch her breath, she said, "Why, Michael, I do believe you like me."

Looking deep into her lovely blue eyes, I said, "Oh, yes, Maeve, very, very much."

Maeve reached up and took my chin in both hands. She spoke slowly and deliberately. "Mike, I think I'm in love with you."

Holding her close, I replied softly, "I sure hope so."

The hopeful look in her eyes almost brought a tear to mine. "You do?"

In a husky voice, I said, "Yes, because I'm pretty sure I'm in love with you."

She pressed her lips to mine and kissed me deeply. Before things could go too far, there was a knock on the door.

Lifting my head, I said, "That's probably the pizza."

"Probably is." Maeve sounded disappointed we'd been interrupted.

"I guess I should go pay him."

"I guess you should." She made no move to release me from our embrace.

The pizza guy knocked again.

"You'll have to let me go."

"I'll have to let you go," she said. Then she started giggling and finally let me go so I could answer the door.

The pizza delivery guy, who I was glad to see worked for Dupree's, stood on the porch waiting patiently.

"I've got a pizza here for a Maeve Dalton. Are you Maeve Dalton?"

I wondered if I really looked like a Maeve to him. "Uh, no, I'm her boyfriend. I'll pay for the pizza."

Rather than handing me the pizza, he looked at me as if trying to remember who I was.

"Don't I know you? Didn't you used to go to Laney?"

I tried to place him. Looking at his shirt, I noticed his nametag said Philip. I felt like I should know him.

"I graduated from Laney, yeah. How much do I owe for the pizza?"

Philip furrowed his brow in concentration for a couple of seconds before he told me, "Six bucks."

I gave him ten dollars and told him to keep the change. Phil smiled broadly as he figured the tip. He touched the brim of his cap in a sloppy salute and left. When he got to his car, Phil turned back, as if still trying to figure out who I was. Shrugging his shoulders, he climbed into his faded yellow Gremlin and drove off.

Maeve had control of her giggles by the time I went back inside. "So, was it the pizza guy?"

"Um hm," I said, holding up the pizza box as proof. "I'm glad you ordered from Dupree's."

She looked at me like I'd cursed. "Is there anyone else in this town who can make a decent pizza?"

Realizing Maeve had no idea how well I knew the Duprees, I chuckled. "No, babe, there's not."

I knew Alfred Dupree well. When I was a kid, he was the manager at the old Linguini Grill. My folks and I ate there often.

Alfred once told us he hoped to open his own pizza place one day. I told my dad I'd like to see that happen. Dad found a location in a building the Coastal Carolina Realty Trust owned and arranged for the Coastal Carolina Small Business Fund to offer Alfred a loan. My involvement was never suggested. Very few people knew that, through my inheritance, I was the actual owner of both the trust and the fund.

"The delivery guy acted like he thought he knew you," Maeve said.

I hadn't realized she was watching. "I think I

looked familiar, but he couldn't place me. He knew we'd gone to Laney together."

Maeve took the pizza box and led the way to the kitchen. "Let's eat while it's still warm."

As I was about to bite into my first slice of the pepperoni, green pepper, and mushroom pizza, Maeve started asking questions.

"Michael, what did you do in the Navy?"

Wanting to answer her question without getting into too much detail, I said, "I drove boats."

Her expression told me that wasn't as detailed an answer as she wanted. "Big boats?"

"No, little boats."

She absorbed that, and when I offered nothing more, she continued. "Why'd you get out of the Navy?"

"I got hurt. My boat was hit by something that made a really big bang. I wound up with a broken hip, among other assorted fractions, abrasions, and contusions. All in all, it was bad enough that when I left the hospital, the Navy kicked me out."

That wasn't the whole story, but it was all I felt ready to tell.

Maeve noticed the trace of regret in my voice. "Did you want to stay in the Navy?"

I set my glass of iced tea on the table and shrugged. "No, not really. The plan was always to do my four years, get out, get married, and go back to college."

Maeve's head snapped up, and I realized I should have been more careful.

"You were planning to get married?" Maeve asked, with an edge to her voice. "May I ask to whom, and what happened?"

Needing a moment to get my thoughts together, I took a healthy swallow of my iced tea. "Do you remember my telling you about my friend Rhiannon?"

Maeve, her expression unreadable, nodded slowly. I gave her a brief version of how I wound up engaged to my best friend, and why I no longer was.

"That's a pretty incredible story, Michael," Maeve said when I was done. "Maybe you should write a book."

I couldn't tell from the look on her face if she was angry or amused. Finally, she asked the question nagging at her most. "Where is Rhiannon now?"

"As far as I know, she's still in Africa digging wells." I sounded as if I didn't really care, which I didn't. "She's no longer part of my life."

Maeve smiled when she heard the finality in my voice. She got up and came around the table to stand beside me. "I'm glad to hear that. And I am sorry you got hurt, Mike, but I'm glad you're here."

She bent down and kissed me. I wasn't sure which hurt she meant. It didn't really matter, as long as she knew I was glad to be there, too.

Eventually, we made it to the library and got some work done. Later in her apartment, over tea, I asked a very important question. "Maeve, when was the last time you went sailing?"

She turned to me with a puzzled look. Not the question she was expecting.

"What in the world does that have to do with anything? I haven't been sailing in years. Why?"

"You know my place on the river up by Camp Riversail? I want you to come with me when I fly home this weekend."

"You fly up there?" Maeve asked. "You still have your plane?"

"Yes, and I still work some weekends at camp as a sailing instructor. Believe it or not, we still use the same old Flying Scotts for our sailing classes. You'd be an old hand."

I studied her face, trying to judge whether she was receptive to the idea.

"If you come up, you can stay at my house. I have an extra bedroom. Or if you'd be more comfortable, you could probably stay at camp. I'd love for you to come up and see the house."

"Wow, that's a lot to take in." Maeve sat back and gave the idea about two seconds' thought. "Yes, Michael, I'd love to see the place where the man I love loves to spend his time. When do we leave?"

"Tomorrow, as soon as you get home from work and get packed." Looking at my watch, I realized how late it was. "I better get going. We've still got to get through tomorrow."

Maeve walked me to the door and kissed me good night. I'd just opened my car door when Kim pulled into the next parking space.

"Well, hello 'That Mike.' How's it going?"

With a big smile, I said, "Better than I ever dared hope."

CHAPTER FIVE

October 1983

Friday passed like slow torture. Each second seemed to take a minute, and each minute an hour. Finally, the day was over, and it was time to pick Maeve up for our escape to River Dream. She was packed and ready when I got to her apartment.

Maeve opened the door just as I was about to knock. For a moment I stood there looking foolish, my hand poised to strike the door. I covered by asking, "So, how was work today?"

She chuckled at my predicament. Reaching out and taking hold of my hand, Maeve pulled me into her arms. After a brief kiss, she answered my question. "It was good; pretty quiet for a Friday."

Her answer seemed distracted. I could tell something was on her mind. She turned and took a couple of steps into the apartment before stopping to face me. "Mike, I've been thinking about Rhiannon."

I lowered my chin and looked at her carefully, trying to read her expression. Her brow was furrowed, and her lips were pressed into a thin line.

"I was wondering what happens to us if she suddenly shows up?"

"What do you mean?" I asked. I thought I had a pretty good idea. We'd talked a good deal about Rhiannon the summer we'd nearly fallen in love the first time.

Maeve knew Rhiannon was more than just a friend to me in those days. And after our talk the night before, she knew we'd been engaged. Apparently, Maeve was worried I might still have feelings for Rhiannon.

Exasperation at my response showed on her face. "What do you mean, what do I mean? If Rhiannon suddenly shows up, will you stay with me, or go back to her?"

Maeve was blunt and to the point as always.

Then it was my turn. "I have no feelings left for Rhiannon," I said, my voice cold and hard. I walked up to Maeve and whispered, "She's my past; you are my future."

"That's right," Maeve said, her eyes flashing. Then her expression softened. "Rhiannon had her chance. Now I have mine. I let you walk away from me once. I was young and didn't know better. But you're my man now. I won't make the same mistake again."

I looked at Maeve, saw the love and determination in her eyes, the tears welling there, and I couldn't hold back. Taking her in my arms, I held her, kissed her, and told her I loved her. Laying her head against my chest, she whispered, "I love you, too, Michael. I love you so much."

When we drove up to my hangar, Maeve commented she'd never seen the general aviation side of an airport before. We parked in the garage attached to the hangar and grabbed our bags. Inside the hangar waited my restored Cessna 170, *Sky Dream*.

Noticing the name stenciled on the nose, Maeve said, "You seem to have a thing for naming stuff after dreams, Mike."

"Yeah, I guess it's kind of a theme with me."

Maeve pointed to the other plane in the hangar. "Whose is that? The one with two engines?"

"That's a Piper Seneca. It's got greater range and carries more passengers than the Cessna, but it can't land at River Dream."

"They're both yours?" Maeve sounded a little skeptical.

Feeling awkward admitting I owned two aircraft, I shrugged and nodded.

Maeve's eyes widened, and she shook her head. "Wow."

"The big one really belongs to the trust. We bought it for me to fly back and forth when I was in the Navy. It's faster and, like I said, has more range than the 170. *Sky Dream*'s my personal plane."

Maeve looked at me curiously. "What's the trust?"

She was beginning to realize the story I gave her at summer camp about inheriting a little money may have left some things out.

"The trust handles all my business investments and stuff like that. My dad oversees the financial part. There's a trustee up in Boston who handles the legal side of things. The trust is set up so the money is there when I need it, but I never have to worry about it."

"So, Mike, back when you told me you'd inherited a *little* money, you were being modest?"

Her tone wasn't quite sarcastic, but her expression told me I needed to elaborate some on just how little money I'd inherited. "It's a long story. Let's get airborne, and I'll try to explain."

After doing the preflight check, I started the engine and taxied out to the threshold. There was a Piedmont flight landing. The tower cleared us for takeoff as soon as it turned onto the taxiway. Once we achieved level flight, Maeve prompted me to finish the story of my little inheritance.

"I'm named after a man named Michael Justin. The Justin part was also in honor of my mother's father. Michael Justin served with my Grandpa Justin Rollings in World War I, in France. Grandpa saved his life, and after the war they stayed friends.

"I don't really remember Mr. Justin. He passed away when I was four, the same year as my mom's momma. That was a tough year for all of us, but especially for Grandpa.

"I know Mr. Justin from the pictures and stories. He was my Godfather. I remember Grandma a little better. She read to me a lot.

"Since Mr. Justin passed away, things with the

trust have been on autopilot, at least from my perspective. I've received a monthly allowance all my life. It goes up every year. From the beginning, the money was more than I needed to get by. So, my dad - and me when I got old enough to understand - invested some and gave some away."

Maeve listened quietly until I finished. "That's the most incredible thing I've ever heard. What about your mom and dad, or your sister? Did they inherit any of it?"

I glanced at her quickly before turning my attention back to flying the plane.

"No, it all went to me. When I was little, my mom and dad received the distributions and used them to take care of me. The trust also paid off the house on Wrightsville Beach. After Grandma died, Grandpa moved in with us. He passed away when I was eight.

"Eventually, I started investing the money from the distributions in businesses on Wrightsville Beach and hired my dad to keep track of it all for me. Then, after I found out I could suggest to the trustee that he invest in certain businesses, I was able to make a real difference. It was all done through third parties and corporations. Most people have no idea I'm involved at all. That's how I want it."

Maeve was quiet for a while. I could tell she was thinking. I was worried about what she was thinking. After a long time, she looked at me and put her hand on my arm.

"You had all that and still didn't turn into some spoiled rich kid. You certainly did a good job keeping it low key."

"My mom and dad had a lot to do with it. They wanted me to have a normal childhood not tainted by the money. At the same time, they used it to make sure I got to do things, like travel, and go to Camp Riversail."

Maeve shook her head in wonder. "And then you went and joined the Navy. Did they know about all the money?"

"I never tried to hide it. I suppose they knew, what with all the background checks they did."

I checked my watch, my instruments, and looked out at the ground below us. We were flying over the river off Oriental.

"Don't look now," I said, "but we overshot the airstrip."

CHAPTER SIX

Maeve's eyes widened with concern. "Is that bad?"

I flashed her a reassuring smile. "Not really, I'll just circle around. We'll fly low over the field, check for obstacles, and see which way the wind is blowing. Then we'll land this puppy."

I brought the plane around and lined up with the grass landing strip. Seeing I wasn't worried reassured Maeve. Her mind went back to my story.

"That's some tale you told me. I understand why you downplayed it before. I probably wouldn't have believed it."

"It's hard for me to believe sometimes, and I've lived it. If I ever started thinking too much of myself because of it all, my folks would remind me I hadn't done anything to earn it. It was all a gift from a very special man whose memory I should honor."

We flew low over the field and saw no obstructions. After noting that the windsock showed a light crosswind, I circled around and came in for a landing. We bounced a little and then were down, coming to a stop well short of the end of the field. I taxied back to the shelter that did duty as a hangar and turned so the tail was pointing into the shelter. After shutting down the motor, I got out, went around, and helped Maeve down.

"Now you get to see some of my fancy equipment in action. Then you can help me tie her down."

"Tie her down?"

"Yeah, once we get her parked under the shelter, we tie her down to make sure the wind doesn't do unpleasant things to her."

"Oh," Maeve replied, still wearing a puzzled expression.

I unlocked the shed next to the shelter and pushed back the door. There were cobwebs between the steering wheel and the seat on the lawn tractor I used for pulling the plane and mowing the runway. I brushed them off before cranking up the tractor.

After driving out and hooking up to the tail wheel, I pulled *Sky Dream* into place. Then, I showed Maeve how to tie the plane down so it would be secure until we flew back to Wilmington on Sunday. With that done, we grabbed our bags, loaded them into the old Jeep, and headed over to camp.

"Aren't we going to the house first?" Maeve asked.

I hadn't said anything to her, but I'd already let Mr. Cooper, the Camp Director, and Captain Jack, the Sailing Master, know Maeve was coming with me.

"I thought we'd do that later, after we get done

at camp. You've been invited to join the campers and crew for dinner at the dining hall."

Most weekends in fall or spring, Camp was reserved by church or youth groups. Occasionally, a family would rent the camp for a big reunion. Maeve's first weekend back at camp was a little different. It was Adult Beginner Sailing School Weekend, a special sailing class for grownups who'd always wanted to learn to sail but never had the chance.

When the campers arrived Friday evening, we checked them in, ate dinner in the dining hall, and then headed out on the water. Early October was still daylight savings time. It stayed light late enough for us to get the aspiring sailors out on the Flying Scotts, nineteen-foot sailboats that were perfect for teaching novices to sail.

We showed them a little of what they'd be learning over the weekend. As luck would have it, Maeve wasn't assigned to my boat. She wound up sailing with my good friend, Chase Arnold. He and I had competed for Maeve's attention that summer we all worked on camp staff.

Chase and I had been coming to Camp Riversail since elementary school. Chase grew up in Apex, North Carolina. He'd been recruited to the College of Charleston Sailing Team. After college, Chase took a job with a computer firm in Research Triangle Park. He came down and helped at camp almost every weekend.

Captain Jack Irving, Camp Riversail's sailing captain, asked if any of our new campers had any sailing experience. He looked over his glasses at Maeve. "I know you know how to sail, missy."

None of the others raised their hands. They were truly novices.

"Good, you're all at the same level starting out then." Jack paused and looked questioningly at Maeve. "Tell me, missy, do you remember how to rig a Scott?"

Over dinner, I'd warned her to expect the question. She was prepared.

"It's been a while, Jack, but I remember."

"Well then, if you're ready to sail a Scott, maybe you should replace one of my mates here." Jack looked at us over the top of his tortoise-shell framed glasses. "They're mostly a bunch of lubbers."

Jack, who'd spent most of his life sailing everything from dinghies to tall ships, considered anyone who spent more than a few days at a time off the water a landlubber. He'd thought of me that way until I came home from the Navy. Jack told me one night after I got home, while we were sitting at the end of my dock drinking iced tea, that I'd earned the right to be called a sailor the hard way.

Maeve laughed too but demurred politely. "I don't know about that. It's been a few years. I haven't had many chances to sail lately."

"Alright then, if you're sure? I'll have to trust these good people to the tender mercies of my crew."

Everyone laughed at that, especially those of us who made up his crew. Jack was good at putting people at ease.

We showed the campers the sailing hut and fitted

them with life jackets before climbing aboard the Scotts. A couple of the instructors had rigged them while the rest of us were eating dinner.

A Scott can be sailed single-handed if it's rigged right. Those at Camp were rigged for a crew of two or more. That let us assign jobs to the campers right away. Nothing fancy, just how to ease and trim the jib sheet. Instructors handled the tiller and mainsheet.

On my boat, I demonstrated raising the mainsail and jib. Then, I talked my fledgling crew through backing the jib as I pushed the tiller over until we were clear of the dock. Finally, I trimmed the mainsail while Ginger Fredericks, who volunteered to be first, trimmed the jib. We eased out onto the river.

The winds were out of the West, Northwest at around six knots, so there wasn't much chop. I steered us on a broad reach, explaining as we went along what I was doing with the tiller, the mainsheet, and what point of sail we were on. After a few minutes, we came about towards the wind and sailed a close reach.

Ginger turned to me with a puzzled expression. "It feels windier suddenly. Why is that?"

"What you're feeling is an effect of apparent wind," I replied, "caused by us sailing into the wind now instead of with it. You'll learn all about apparent wind this weekend."

The sound of an air horn caught our attention, and we looked toward Camp. There stood Captain Jack, signaling us to return to the dock. Reluctantly, we came about and headed back.

Once all the boats were tied up at the dock, we

showed the campers how to de-rig the boats. They helped carry the sails up to the sail loft before we dismissed them. After the campers left for their cabins, we returned to the dock to move the boats to their moorings for the night. Before the staff could call it a night, we met with Captain Jack to go over the next day's agenda and assignments. Satisfied we all knew the plan; he told us to call it a night.

Most of the staff stayed on camp. Some who lived nearby, like me, headed for home.

"That was fun," Maeve said as we climbed into the Jeep. "I'd forgotten how much I like sailing."

The Jeep was an old blue CJ-7 with a soft top and no doors. It had doors, but I only put them on when the weather turned cold or wet.

I squeezed Maeve's hand and smiled. "I'm glad you enjoyed it. I wish Captain Jack had put you on my boat. Then again, maybe it's better he didn't. I might've ignored the others on board."

Maeve shook her head, but she was smiling. "I saw your place from the river. The old cottage is gone, huh?"

I noted a hint of regret in her voice, or perhaps it was nostalgia. "It was taken down after the house was finished."

She nodded her understanding. "Was that your sailboat out in front, up on the lift?"

"She was. She's mine. I don't get to sail her much these days. She's a Hunter 26. She's kind of big for a day sail, but just right for a long weekend out on the Sound. I got her last summer."

"Do you still have *Riverscape*?" She sounded worried that I might not.

"You may not have seen her. She's tied up between the Hunter and the shore."

Maeve was the first person to sail aboard *Riverscape* with me. She'd given me the idea for the name.

Maeve shook her head but smiled. "No, I didn't see her. I did see a powerboat tied up on the other side."

"That's my fishing boat. It's a 20' Grady-White. They're made right here in North Carolina, you know."

"So, you're a sailor and a motorboater. Do you row, too?" Maeve asked with a laugh.

"Not athletic-style rowing, but I do have a canoe, and I know how to paddle a kayak."

She put her hands behind her head and stretched before saying, "A very versatile man on the water, aren't you?"

We arrived at the house, and I carried her bag inside. The front porch was screened in so folks could sit out there and enjoy watching the river without uninvited little guests on wings.

The house faced the river but was across the road from the riverbank. That wasn't a big deal since the only traffic on the road was me or people coming to see me. There weren't any other houses at my end of the road.

I unlocked the front door, took Maeve's hand, and gave her the nickel tour. From the front door, a hallway ran the length of the house to the back door.

Immediately inside the door on the left was a coat

closet and then the living room. Across the hall from the living room was the front bedroom.

In the living room was a wood stove, framed by two windows looking upriver towards Camp Riversail. A double doorway opened from the living room into the dining room, which was the same size as the living room.

The left wall of the dining room had a double bay window. The window was flanked by built-in hutches for dinnerware and such. They could do duty as bookcases. Through the dining room was another double door opening into the kitchen. Each double doorway had disappearing doors that could be pulled out to close off the living room, the kitchen, or both. The kitchen was the biggest room in the house.

When Maeve asked why, I said, "I did it to accommodate a large breakfast nook since I figured I'd probably use the dining room for something else and wind up eating all my meals in the kitchen. So far, the kitchen and the bedrooms are the only fully furnished rooms in the house."

Along the interior wall of the kitchen was a walk-in pantry. Just before the back door on the left was a half-bath, and across the hall from that was the laundry closet. The back door led out onto a screened porch and then into the backyard. The yard was small as I didn't want to have to spend a lot of time tending to it. It blended along its edges into the surrounding field I was allowing to go fallow.

We went back into the house, and I showed Maeve the den, which was across the hall from the dining room, setting her bag down outside the door of and bypassing the main bedroom and bath for the moment. The den was furnished simply, with just a desk, a folding table, and a filing cabinet.

"This is where I study when I'm here."

In the front inside corner of the den was a small bathroom with a shower stall, accessible from the den or the front bedroom. The front bedroom was furnished with the double bed, nightstand, and chest of drawers that were in my bedroom in the old cottage.

"I haven't gotten around to picking out a new bedroom suite yet. Maybe you could help with that?"

We made our way to the main bedroom. I picked up her bag as we entered.

So that the main bedroom and bath could be larger, the front bedroom and the den were smaller than the living and dining rooms. The main bedroom was furnished with a maple bedroom set including a queen-sized bed with bookcase headboard, a matching chest of drawers, and a mirrored dresser. The matching drapes and bedspread were earth tones with just a hint of green sprinkled throughout.

"Michael, it's beautiful. The whole house is beautiful. It's like a fairy tale cottage. I love it."

Then I showed Maeve the *pièce de résistance* - the main bathroom. I'd given this room a lot of thought.

The toilet itself was in an alcove that could be closed off from the rest of the bathroom. A large vanity with double sinks sported two ornately framed mirrors, each bracketed by hundred-watt lights in wrought iron fixtures. In the back corner along the outside wall was a separate shower stall.

The centerpiece was a large garden tub. It was not just a tub, but a Jacuzzi tub, located directly under a large skylight. The skylight was vented so as not to steam up, and on a clear night you could see the stars.

We stood in the doorway for a moment before Maeve turned to me. "You've really built yourself one special home here, Mike, a lovely home."

"It's a home now that I have a lovely lady to share it with. It's our home, baby. I'm glad you like it."

Maeve moved into my arms. "I don't just like it, sweetie, I love it, and I love you."

Our kiss was on the verge of becoming something more when she pulled gently away. "I better unpack."

Taking a deep breath, I let it out slowly and said, "I'll go put the kettle on."

Later, we went out on the front porch on the swing I'd moved to the house from the cabin, to enjoy the night sounds of the river and sip our tea.

"I can see why you love it here, Mike. I've fallen in love with this place, and I've only been here a few hours. How can you stand to be away from here?"

Sometimes I wondered about that myself. "I know it's always here waiting for me. This spot is special to me, even more special now that you're here to share it with."

Maeve made a contented sigh and snuggled against me. It started getting chilly, and I felt her shiver.

"You know," I said, "we've got to be up early, and it's

going to be a long day tomorrow. Maybe we ought to think about going in."

Maeve agreed. We reluctantly left the porch for the warmth of the house and our bed.

CHAPTER SEVEN

October 1983

The smell of fresh coffee brewing woke me up just before dawn the next morning. Maeve was up already. Slipping into my robe, I walked over to the kitchen and found a fresh pot of coffee on, but no Maeve. After filling my mug, I headed out to the porch and found my love curled up on the porch swing sipping from her cup.

"It's so lovely here, Michael. I just wanted to sit and watch the sunrise from our swing. Yes, love, I recognized this swing. It's the swing we're we first -"

I joined her on the swing and kissed her, interrupting what she'd been about to say. After the kiss, she leaned over so our shoulders touched, and we watched dawn spread light over the river. The beauty of the moment made my heart swell.

"Michael, tell me we can stay here forever. Tell me we'll never have to leave."

"Babe, we can stay here forever. If you really wish it, we really can."

Maeve turned those beautiful blue eyes up to me, eyes full of love for me and for the moment.

"And you could make it happen, couldn't you? And you'd do it for me, wouldn't you? But that would be selfish of us, of me. I have a goal I want to reach. And you, I know you want to finish school, study the sea. It's your dream. You're a natural on the water, Mike. I saw it when I watched you sailing yesterday. You belong out there. And I want to go there with you."

"You can, Maeve. I can't imagine going without you."

We shared a gentle kiss, and then sensible Maeve returned.

"We should get over to camp before we miss breakfast."

After breakfast, the campers spent time in class getting their book learning before going out on the boats to try what they'd been taught. Again, Captain Jack assigned Maeve and me to different boats, but I didn't mind. Jack knew what he was doing.

We made sure each crew could rig the boat and raise the sails before we headed out onto the river. Each budding sailor took a turn at the helm, worked the mainsheet, and worked the jib sheets. Before we knew it, the lunch horn sounded. We headed in, tied up, furled the sails, and made our way to the dining hall.

Maeve waited for me on the dock. Mine was the last boat in. I did this by design. It meant more time on the water, even if only a minute or two. Maeve and I walked together, but upon reaching the dining hall, she sat at her crew table, and I sat at mine. Captain Jack preferred crews dined together.

Lunch was followed by a free period before the next classroom session. Some campers headed off to their cabins for a quick nap. Several joined some of the staff at the picnic tables outside the dining hall. We discussed what they'd learned so far and what to expect that afternoon.

Those discussions were my favorite part of the Adult Class. Teaching kids to sail is fun and rewarding in its own way, but I enjoyed the Adult Sailing weekends as the conversations were much different and the questions much more on point.

Break time ended. The campers, including Maeve, who felt she could use the refresher, headed to class. The rest of us headed to the dock to check on the boats. We spent the time discussing the campers.

We all agreed it was a pretty good group, better than most we'd had. They listened to us and gave us credit for knowing what we were doing. They also asked intelligent questions. Chase and I moved off for a little conversation of our own.

Standing at the end of the Riversail dock, I noted a light breeze coming out of the northwest and thought it would be an enjoyable afternoon for sailing. Chase's mind wasn't on the sailing conditions.

"Mike, man, Maeve is still hot."

I couldn't argue with that.

"Not only that, she still knows how to handle a

Scott. She needs to be on the sailing staff."

Coming from Chase, that was high praise.

"I hope Captain Jack agrees with you. I think she'd like that."

Then Chase sprang his news on me. "Y'all are going to need somebody. This is my last weekend for a while."

"What! Why is that, Chase?"

"School, man," Chase said. "A master's degree is more work than I thought it would be. It's getting tough coming all the way down here from Raleigh on so many weekends. Dude, we don't all have private planes."

I know he didn't mean it to, but that stung. "Hey, Chase, I'll fly up to RDU and pick you up if it'll help."

Chase turned from looking out over the river. "I know you would, Mike, but that's not the big reason."

An uncharacteristically shy smile crossed his face. "I've met someone. If I'm down here every other weekend I'm not with her, you see?"

I understood. It was a girl, not the books.

"Her name is Alexa. She's in her senior year at State and is really serious about her studies. She thinks I should be too. She's right about that. I should be. I'm not off to such a great start."

Punching Chase playfully on the shoulder, I laughed. "It sounds like she's a good influence on you."

Chase's smile broadened. "You know it, Mike. I told Captain Jack last night. He was understanding about it all. He told me I'm welcome back anytime I can make it."

I glanced up the dock as if expecting to see our sailing captain coming our way. "That's cool. Jack's a pretty good skipper."

"Yeah, he is."

Following my gaze, Chase saw our charges returning for their next excursion on the river. It was their turn to rig the boats themselves under our watchful eyes. Our job was to make sure they didn't do anything dangerous.

All went well, and soon we were tacking and jibing back and forth across the river. Our time on the river always seemed too short. When we got back to the dock, we could proudly report that all our students successfully completed the tasks set for them. Besides, everyone was getting hungry for supper.

Supper was fried chicken with mashed potatoes and corn on the cob, followed by chocolate cake with vanilla ice cream. They fed us well at camp. A short break followed dinner, and then it was back on the water.

When sailing upwind, if the bow points directly into the wind, the boat stops. Sailors call this getting into irons. We practiced getting in and out of irons until the sun started to disappear behind Cherry Branch.

As dusk fell, it was back to the dock. The campers de-rigged the boats and got them set for the night. While they carried the sails to the loft, the staff moved the boats out to their moorings. Then it was up to the loft to help stow the sails, and we were done for the day. The campers headed into Oriental to check out the lounge at the Marina. The staff headed for home.

Maeve's eyes sparkled with excitement. She jumped into the Jeep, showing no signs of sharing the fatigue I was feeling.

"Today was such a great day. Carol and Eddie got the hang of things right off. Chase is a great instructor. He's really changed since Camp."

Her enthusiasm was infectious, and I had to smile. "He had some nice things to say about you, too."

Maeve cocked her head and raised her eyebrow. "Oh, such as?"

"He said you really knew your way around a Scott and should be working as an instructor. In fact, he recommended you to replace him. Oh, he also thinks you're hot."

"Replace him, why?" She pointedly did not respond to the hot reference, though I noticed a quick smile cross her face.

In a very serious voice, I told her. "He says that due to obligations at home, he will have to curtail his sailing instructor duties at Camp for an indefinite period."

"Chase said that?" she asked, rolling her eyes playfully.

"Well, not exactly," I said. "He's met a girl and wants to spend more time studying her. I mean studying with her on the weekends."

"He'll be studying with her, and studying her, if I know him. I'm glad he's found someone. He'll be missed around here, though."

"Yes, he will. He's our best instructor after Captain

Jack."

"Even better than you?" Maeve asked with a mischievous smile.

"Chase is better than me by a long shot. He's a skilled sailor. That's why he was on the team at C of C with a full ride."

"I didn't know about the scholarship," Maeve said. "I mean, he told us he was on the sailing team at the College of Charleston, but he didn't elaborate."

By now we'd been sitting in the driveway for several minutes.

Maeve swung her legs around and jumped out of the Jeep. Looking over her shoulder at me, she asked, "Don't you think we ought to go in?"

"It would probably be a good idea. I don't know about you, but I could use a shower."

We needed to wash off the accumulated spray from a day on the water. After our showers, we spent some time on the front porch, enjoying the night sounds on the river.

"You can tell fall is upon us. The night air is saying so," I said.

"That's rather poetic, Mike," Maeve said. "You're right, though. There's a chill in the air tonight. But it's snuggly warm on this porch swing with you."

CHAPTER EIGHT

Sunday mornings were always the most fun morning of weekend sailing school. After a sunrise prayer service and breakfast, we took the campers down to the beach for capsize recovery training. They received a brief class on the theory of how to right a capsized sailboat and then boarded the Aqua Finns.

Aqua Finns are small one- or two-person sailboats with single sails. Jack had each instructor take out one camper at a time. We went out a little way and capsized the boats. In order to qualify at this task, the new sailors had to successfully right the boat in shallow water, and then again in water over their heads. Everybody got dunked.

Captain Jack quizzed Maeve on the process. Convinced she remembered how to right an Aqua Finn, he put her to work as an instructor for the capsize drill. Jack did this for two reasons. First, it allowed us to put the campers through the exercise more quickly and, second, it gave him a chance to see how Maeve might do as an instructor.

Since she'd been crewing with Carol and Eddie, Jack asked if they'd mind having Maeve put them through the capsize drill.

Eddie looked at Carol and smiled. "We don't mind. From what she's told us; it won't be the first time Maeve's capsized a sailboat."

"Hey," Maeve complained, "only Aqua Finns, and I always managed to right them."

Chase looked at me, grinned, and said, "With just a little help."

Maeve gave him a sour look, and replied, "Sometimes very little."

When she saw the hurt look on Chase's face, she laughed. "Yes, Chase, you were always there to rescue me."

Seeing I was about to protest, she added, "And you, too, Mike. These two would knock each other out to see who got to rescue me first."

Captain Jack shook his head and laughed along with her. "I remember that well."

Giving me a sly wink, he added, "I guess we know who finally came out ahead there, don't we?"

I wisely kept my mouth shut and just smiled. Maeve turned an interesting shade of red.

Deciding things had gone far enough in that direction, Jack steered us back on course.

"It's settled then. Carol and Eddie will do their capsizing with Maeve, since they acknowledge she's something of an expert in tipping over sailboats." He held his hand up as Maeve started to protest. "And in setting them to rights again. So, let's get started."

We made quite a game of it and practiced more than just the requisite two drills. Then the campers took turns sailing the little boats around in the protected area right off the beach.

After lunch came the most serious lesson - the crew-overboard drill. For this, we moved back onto the Flying Scotts. As we didn't want to risk anyone getting run over by the boats, we used anchored buoys in place of overboard crew members.

Captain Jack's tone was serious as he instructed the campers. "The key to retrieving an overboard crew member is to sail towards his position on a point perpendicular to the wind and then turn abruptly into the wind while coming alongside the person in the water. Getting it right takes a lot of practice."

Once the novice sailors showed they could stop the boat next to the buoy, they faced the real test. The staff member on their boat threw out a flotation cushion and cried, "Crew overboard!" with no warning. The student sailors would have to come about and sail back to recover the cushion, which, of course, was not anchored in place. It took some of them several tries, but eventually they all got it right.

Having rescued all the errant cushions, it was time for the final lesson, bringing the boat into the dock. The campers had learned how to sail away from the dock the previous afternoon. Part one of the crew-overboard drills helped prepare them for this exercise.

It wasn't long before everyone managed to bring their boats in without banging the dock too hard. Captain Jack declared success.

We de-rigged the boats and secured the sails in the sail loft. The campers gathered in the screened-in classroom for some last words of sailing wisdom from Captain Jack. Before they left, he signed off on their US Sailing Small Boat Sailor Certifications, better known as Red Books, showing they'd successfully completed all the light air and most of the heavy air requirements.

In closing, Jack invited everyone to come back to the Family Sailing Camp in two weeks.

"Even if you don't have a family to bring, you're all part of our Camp family now and more than welcome. With luck, we'll have heavier air, and you can finish off your Red Books."

Addresses and phone numbers were exchanged. Promises were made to keep in touch. Many campers said they'd try to come back for the Family Camp.

Once the campers had packed up and driven off, the staff, including Maeve, met with Captain Jack in the dining hall. We discussed how the class had gone and how we could make the next class even better.

Then it was time to go. Leaving camp was always a sad time for me. I enjoyed working with the people there. Maeve and I went back to River Dream to pack up and put the house in order before heading back to Wilmington. Before we left, there was one thing she insisted we do.

"Mike, we haven't even taken a walk on the dock to

see *Riverscape*," she said. "Let's do that before we leave."

I couldn't deny her that, so out onto the dock we went.

"She sure looks lonely, doesn't she?" Maeve said as we stood on the dock next to *Riverscape*. "Do we have time to go aboard for a minute?"

In reply, I reached down and loosened the line holding the corner of the tarp covering the cockpit. Once it was back far enough, Maeve climbed aboard.

"This sure brings back memories. Mike, you'll never know how often I've thought back to the time we spent on board *Riverscape* that summer." Almost more to herself than to me, she added, "You'll never know how much I missed you."

Unsure if she meant me or the boat, I joined her in the cockpit. "You don't have to miss me anymore, babe. I'm right here, and we're back aboard *Riverscape*."

That she'd even thought about me in the years since that summer both surprised and pleased me. I put my arms around her and hugged her close.

"Dear God, please don't let this be a dream," Maeve whispered into my chest.

"It's no dream," I assured her.

I didn't want the moment to end, but we needed to get in the air.

"Babe, I hate to break the mood, but we should get going."

"I know," Maeve said. She let me go and climbed back onto the dock.

I secured the tarp and caught up with her at the door to the screen room. Just as I reached her, she opened the door and stepped inside. Looking at the swing, she said, "That swing is where it happened, Mike? It's where we first made love."

The memory of that night on the swing, the day we brought *Riverscape* home, came flooding back.

"Yes, babe, it happened right there," I said.

She took my hand and pulled me to the swing. We sat down.

"Are you just going to sit there, or are you going to kiss me?" Maeve said, in an echo of that night long ago.

The late afternoon rays of autumn sunshine lit her hair, and in the playful smile on her face I saw the girl I'd first kissed on that swing. The same wave of desire I'd felt then swept over me again. I pressed my lips to hers, hungry for the feel of her mouth on mine, want for her surging like a storm tide inside me. It was a moment I hoped would never end.

"The last time we were here, I wasn't smart enough to know to hold on to you, Michael. I'm a lot smarter now."

Maeve seemed satisfied she'd corrected the mistake she'd made that summer. She stood up and took my hand. We walked back across the road to the Jeep. A few minutes later, the Jeep was parked safely back in the shed. I pulled the Cessna out onto the strip, checked the wind, and we took off.

"I'm really going to miss it," Maeve said.

"We can come back next week, every weekend, anytime you want. It's your home now, too."

"It really is. It feels like I've finally come home to the home I've been waiting to find."

Maeve turned to me with a serene look on her face. "Does that make any sense?"

"It makes perfect sense to me," I said. We flew on in silence for a few minutes, lost in our thoughts.

Out of the blue, Maeve asked, "By the way, Mike, how much do you get paid for working at Camp?"

I laughed. "Why do you ask?"

"Well, when Captain Jack asked me to join the staff, he said he thought I was worth at least twice what he pays you, maybe more. I told him that it was very nice of him to say so, but he should just pay me whatever starting rate he pays his regular staff. He said he'd do that and laughed. Come to think of it, he never told me how much."

By then, it was all I could do to keep the plane in level flight, as I was wracked with a fit of laughter.

Maeve pressed her lips into a thin line and glared at me. "What are you laughing about?"

With a manly effort, I brought it under control. "Babe, it's a good thing you didn't agree to take two or three times my pay."

"And why not?" she replied coldly.

"Because, sweetheart, I don't get paid for working at camp. I volunteer."

Maeve sputtered, her face twisting with indignation. "Why that, why you, you could have said something."

I tried to be serious but couldn't keep the smile off my face.

"You never asked. Maeve, the sailing school is funded by an endowment set up by my trust years ago. That's how they're able to keep the registration fee so low. The boats, equipment, and staff are all paid for from the endowment. The only things we really charge the campers for are their meals, textbooks, and Red Books."

Maeve pursed her lips and looked thoughtfully out the windscreen for a few minutes. Finally, she turned those beautiful heather blue eyes back on me and said, "Okay, I guess that's a good thing. But since I'm your girlfriend, maybe I should just volunteer, too. I'd feel funny knowing I was getting paid, even indirectly, by you. You know what I mean?"

"Yeah, I do. If that's how you want to work it, I'm sure Jack won't object."

I thought it was best not to point out that she was paid that way those summers she worked as a counselor.

"Now, enough about that. It's time for your first flying lesson."

Maeve looked stunned. "What, no, Mike, no!"

CHAPTER NINE

October 1983

I wasn't smiling when I said, "Yes, Maeve, yes. If you're going to fly with me, you need to know the basics, just in case."

"Just in case ... what?" she asked.

"Just in case, for some reason, I need you to fly the airplane."

I could tell from her expression she was still dubious. "Say, like when, for instance?"

"Say, like when I forget to go to the little boys room before takeoff and have to sneak behind the seats to use the relief bottle, just as a for instance."

Maeve wrinkled her nose, but a smile flickered across her lips. "A relief bottle, that's gross. Can't you just put the plane on autopilot or something?"

"Babe, this little plane doesn't have an autopilot. Besides, I think you'll enjoy flying once you get the hang of it. It's kind of like sailing, only in 3-D."

With an odd look of determination, Maeve said, "Okay, I'll give it a try. On one condition."

"What?" I asked.

Maeve laughed. "You never forget to go before we take off. The idea of the relief bottle is just gross."

"It's a deal. Now, put your hands on the yoke - the steering thing there - and your feet on the rudder pedals. That's it."

So began Maeve's first unofficial flying lesson. Unofficial due to the fact that I was not a certified flight instructor. Once she got a feel for it, she started enjoying it.

I had her bank to the left and right and use the rudder to turn, tried to explain all the dials and gauges, and had her gain and lose altitude. As we approached Wilmington Airport, I took over. She wasn't quite ready to try an approach and landing.

Once we were on the ground and the plane was secured, I remembered my folks expected us for dinner at seven.

"Maeve, I know this is short notice, but how would you feel about having dinner with my folks in, say, about an hour?"

The look she gave me could not be described as happy. "Short notice! I'll say."

She gestured with both hands at her outfit, a gray UNCW sweatshirt and a worn pair of jeans. "Mike, I can't go to your folks looking like this."

"You look great to me. But we do have an hour, more or less. They don't eat dinner on Sundays until about seven. It's kind of a family tradition."

Maeve gave me an exasperated look and then mellowed. "Okay, Mike. Let's go have dinner with your family after we stop by my apartment so I can freshen up some."

Kim was at home when we got there. She asked how our weekend went. I filled her in while Maeve disappeared down the hall to freshen up.

Maeve came out a short time later, looking wonderful in a white cotton blouse with a pale pink flower pattern on the collar, a tan, knee-length skirt, and a pair of slingback sandals. We told Kim we were on our way to my folks' place for dinner.

Kim shook her head in wonder. "You guys never stop moving, do you? Dinner with the folks, Maeve? Sounds like things are getting serious."

After checking to see if I was paying attention, Maeve leaned in close to Kim. "I think just maybe they are."

"You don't waste time, do you, girl?" Kim said. "Then again, I guess you've waited for this chance for a while."

Maeve arched her brow and nodded at her friend. "Just wish me luck in making a good impression on his folks."

"Good luck, girl. I don't think you'll need it. Once they see how Mike looks at you, they'll know it's true love. Go get 'em."

I reminded them I was right there and suggested we should get going.

On the way to my folks' place, Maeve brought up a pertinent point. "Mike, just what, if anything, have you told your folks about us?"

"During my weekly visits home, I told my mom I'd run into someone from my camp counselor days. Someone I'd had a big crush on is what I told her. And much to my delight, it turns out she liked me too. Of course, Mom asked me who. I told her, Maeve Dalton."

Maeve laughed. "Just like that? Did she have any idea who I was?"

"Just like that," I said. "My mother may surprise you. She has a remarkable memory."

"And what did she say?" Maeve asked.

"I quote, 'Is she not the young lady who sailed *Riverscape* home with you?' To which I replied, 'As a matter of fact, she is.' To which dear old mom replied, 'Well, I can understand you having a crush on her, but what did she see in you?' I told you my mom's good at keeping my ego in check."

Maeve was still chuckling. "Your mom said all that, just like that?"

"Wait 'til you get to know my mom. She always talks that way. I think it has something to do with her growing up as a Yankee."

With two minutes to spare, we pulled up to the house at Wrightsville Beach. My little sister Malori was waiting for us on the deck. Malori, eleven years younger than me, was 11 years old. She shared my slate-blue eyes, and her long brown hair was a shade or two lighter than my own.

Malori was tall for her age and slender. Always active, she loved horseback riding, swimming, and sailing. Seeing my GTO pull into the driveway with the top down, she hollered out, "Mom, Michael's here, and he's got some girl with him."

Maeve gave me a look.

I said, "Kid sister, whatcha gonna do?"

I went around the car and opened Maeve's door. We started walking up the stairs, but by then my dad was coming down the steps to greet us. It was part of being a Southern Gentleman from the old school, I suppose.

Dad took her hand and said, "You must be Maeve. I'm Michael's father, Owen Lanier. We've been looking forward to meeting you. Mrs. Lanier's cooked up something special for tonight's dinner."

Maeve seemed taken with my father's Southern charm. "Thank you, sir. I take it I was expected."

"Well, of course. When his mother told Michael last week that he should invite you, he assured her he would."

Maeve smiled at my dad. "What do you know about that? He just mentioned it to me about an hour ago, after we landed."

I stood there trying to look innocent. My dad turned a disapproving stare on me and then returned his attention to Maeve. "You'll have to forgive my son. He can be absent-minded about some things."

Malori, evidently deciding she'd waited patiently behind our father long enough, pushed past him down the steps.

"Yeah, especially anything that doesn't involve a sail or a rudder. I'm Malori, by the way. Mike's little sister. I figured I'd better introduce myself. No one else seemed to be getting around to it."

For years after I was born, my mom and dad didn't think they'd be able to have any more children. Then along came Malori. Malori shared my blue eyes, but hers always seemed to sparkle with mischief, especially where I was concerned. She apparently felt it was her duty in life to embarrass me. She did it well, too.

Maeve chuckled at Malori's forthrightness. "Hi, Malori, I'm Maeve."

"So, you're my brother's new girlfriend. You're much prettier than his last one," Malori said, surprising me. She'd always liked Rhiannon.

Maeve took it in stride. "Why thank you, Malori."

"Now, Malori, behave yourself," my dad said. He motioned for Maeve and me to go on up the stairs. "Y'all, I think it's time we went into the house. Mike's mother will be starting to wonder if I expect her to serve dinner here in the driveway."

He held Malori back for what I suspected would be a quick discussion about behaving herself in front of guests.

When she wasn't trying to get under my skin, Malori was a sweet kid, and exceedingly smart. She'd skipped a few grades and was already a high school freshman. At the rate she was going, I joked that she'd graduate college before I did.

My parents' house, the house I grew up in, was on the sound side of Wrightsville Beach near the South End. The house part was two-and-a-half stories, but the building was actually three-and-a-half stories high. Like most of the surrounding places, the house itself was raised on pilings. The underside was used for storage and parking.

Originally, the house was owned for me by my trust. When I took control of the trust after being discharged from the Navy, I sold it to my folks for what lawyers call a legally sufficient amount.

Honorable discharge from military service was one of the conditions that could trigger the assets of the trust being turned over to me. The others included marriage, college graduation, or reaching age twenty-five, whichever came first. Since I had no idea how to manage those assets, I immediately hired the trustee as my financial manager under the same basic arrangement as the original trust.

Maeve reached the top of the steps and walked out onto the deck. She stopped to admire the view across the sound. "You woke up to this view every morning growing up?"

I put my arm around her and breathed deeply of the fresh salt air. "Yeah, I never got tired of it either. After Grandpa died, I moved up into the loft. My bedroom window overlooked this same view, only it's even better from up there."

"I'd like to see that," Maeve said, a suggestive gleam in her eyes.

I tightened my arm to pull her closer, kissed her on the head, and then laughed. "You'll have to ask Malori; it's her room now."

Maeve pursed her lips and punched me lightly in the chest. "I'll just do that then," she said before breaking into a giggle.

Dad finished whatever he was saying to Malori, and they started up the steps.

I nodded over my shoulder toward the door. "We'd better get inside. Mom's waiting."

From the deck, a sliding glass door opened into the living room. The living room ran nearly the width of the house. The centerpiece of the room was a glass-topped, oak-wood coffee table my mother was very attached to. It was handmade by a New Hampshire artisan she'd grown up with. The glass top was laser etched with a picture of the covered bridge in Jackson, New Hampshire.

The dining area, to the right of the living room, had a light fixture made from a ship's wheel suspended over an oak dining table that could seat up to eight. It was set for five.

Taking in the place settings on the table, Maeve whispered to me, "I see there's a place set for me. What if I hadn't come?"

I chewed my lower lip as I thought about that. "I'd be in deep trouble."

The galley-style kitchen was separated from the dining area by a breakfast bar. My mother was in the kitchen putting the finishing touches on dinner. She really was a skilled cook.

Thinking I was catching her by surprise, I leaned over the breakfast bar and called out, "Hey Mom! I'm home!"

"I am quite aware of that, son. Your sister announced it loud enough that all the neighbors know it, too, I am certain. And who is this pretty young lady with you?"

Unlike my dad, my mom, though she knew full well this pretty young lady must be Maeve, wouldn't acknowledge it until I made formal introductions.

"Mom, this pretty young lady is Maeve Dalton. Maeve, may I introduce my mother, Eunice Lanier."

"It is a pleasure to meet you, Mrs. Lanier," Maeve said very properly. I thought she sounded a little nervous.

My mom gave her an appraising look, smiled, and stepped forward. "The first thing you are going to have to do, young lady, is call me Eunice. Welcome to our home."

My mother gave Maeve a hug. I looked around to see if I was in the right house. My mother wasn't known for being a hugger. Hearing Dad and Malori coming through the door, I shot him a questioning glance. He just shrugged his shoulders.

Then I heard my mom say to Maeve, "Second thing, young lady, do you know your way around a kitchen?"

Maeve smiled and seemed to relax. "I can usually boil water without burning it and maybe scramble an egg."

A warm smile touched my mother's lips. She put her hand gently on Maeve's arm.

"That is good enough for me, dear. Please, Maeve, will you give me a hand finishing up dinner?"

"I would love to, Eunice," Maeve said.

Malori, Dad, and I all looked at each other, dumbstruck. My mom never allowed anyone to help her in the kitchen.

Leaning in close to my father, I said, "Okay, Dad, who is that woman and what have you done with my mother?"

He gave me a confused look. "I don't know, son. I'm just as surprised as you are. There must be something about Maeve your mom took an instant liking to."

Malori chimed in. "You can say that again. I've never seen Mom act like that. She's never invited any of my friends to help out in the kitchen."

"You people quit jabbering. Michael, come in here and get everyone something to drink. Malori, come take these bowls out to the table. Owen, find something helpful to do."

I could tell by the look on Maeve's face that she enjoyed watching my mom giving us orders.

Dad decided the most helpful thing he could do was retire to the living room and put some background music on the stereo. The rest of us did as Mom directed. Promptly, we were seated at the table, the blessing said, enjoying Mom's chicken a la king.

"Mrs. Lanier, this chicken is wonderful. I don't think I've ever had anything quite like it. It's delicious."

Mom smiled warmly at Maeve. "Thank you, dear. It is a recipe my mother passed along to me. I will be glad to give you a copy."

When she offered to give Maeve her recipe, the rest of us nearly fell out of our seats.

Maeve offered to help clean up after dinner.

My mom had a better idea. "I believe that since we

prepared the meal, the rest of the family can handle the cleaning up. We, my dear, will enjoy a nice glass of iced tea out on the deck, while they take care of things in here."

Flashing me a triumphant grin, Maeve accompanied Mom outside.

Watching them take their seats on the deck, Dad said, "Well, Michael, if you had any worries about whether your mom was going to like Maeve, I think you can put them to rest."

Nodding, I replied, "I guess so. It makes me wonder, though. They just met, and they're carrying on like old friends."

"Don't complain, Mike," Malori said. "Just be glad they're getting along. After all, if you and Maeve are going to be together, isn't it better that Mom likes her?"

Leave it to Malori to put it in the simplest terms.

"I suppose you're right, Mal," I said, giving her shoulder an affectionate tap.

She punched me back and said, "Of course I'm right. I'm much smarter than you are, you know." No false humility there.

In response, I blew dish soap bubbles in her hair. My dad stopped her from retaliating with the sprayer. We finished cleaning up and joined my mom and Maeve on the deck.

"Michael, you did not mention Maeve plays the piano," my mother said as I sat down beside Maeve.

"I didn't know that Maeve plays the piano," I replied truthfully.

With an exasperated shake of her head, my mom asked, "How could you not know a thing like that?"

"She didn't include it on her resume when she applied to be my girlfriend," I said.

Maeve's glare let me know I was going to pay for that.

"Very cute," my mother shot back. "Well, now you know. When we get back from our boat ride, Maeve and I may spend some time in the music room."

My mother's music room was Malori's old bedroom. In it sat a piano, a small organ, and shelf after shelf of sheet music.

"We're going on a boat ride?" I asked. "Isn't it a little late for that?"

"I asked Maeve if she enjoyed cruising the sound at night and watching the lights reflecting on the water. Astonishing me, she said she had never been."

My mother looked at me as if it were my fault Maeve had missed out on such a sight. "I suggested we could take her. Owen, the Whaler is ready to go, is it not?"

"At your command, dear. Who would you like at the helm?" Dad asked with an exaggerated bow.

Mom gave Dad a patient smile. "You are very droll, Owen. Maeve, Owen thinks he is a regular British comedian. He loves Benny Hill and Monty Python.

"I think Malori should drive. She knows the sound best, after Michael, and he will be busy pointing out the sites to Maeve."

"Cool, I love cruising the sound at night," Malori said.

With that decision, we made our way to the dock and boarded my dad's Boston Whaler. His Whaler was a thirty-two-foot, center-console, open-bow, offshore fishing boat with twin one hundred and fifty horsepower Johnson motors on the back. He'd outfitted it with all the latest electronics and fishing equipment. Fortunately, all that fishing gear was safely stored ashore.

Malori, at eleven, could expertly handle our dad's boat. Settling in at the controls, she started the starboard engine.

At Dad's suggestion, Malori ran only one engine for our little cruise. We were staying in the Sound and wouldn't have a need for speed. Once Dad and I cast off the lines, Malori maneuvered away from the dock and into the channel.

From her position near the bow, Maeve said, "You really know what you're doing, Malori."

Malori shrugged, but I could tell by the look on her face that Maeve's words pleased her. She turned the wheel to point our bow more down the middle of the channel before replying.

"Being Mike's little sister, I've spent a lot of time on boats. Michael started teaching me to sail about the time I learned to walk."

Maeve gave me a knowing look and smiled.

"Maeve here is quite a sailor," I said. "Captain Jack was so impressed he offered her a job on the sailing staff."

"Is that right?" my dad said. "You must have really shown old Jack something. He's not easily impressed."

"You have done a lot of sailing then, Maeve?" my mother asked.

"I spent a lot of summers at Camp Riversail when I was a kid," Maeve told them. "When it comes to sailing, Mike and his friend Chase taught me most of what I know."

My mom lifted her gaze and scrunched her brow. Turning to look at Maeve, she said, "Michael told me you are the young lady from camp who helped him sail his boat home."

"Yes, ma'am, that was me," Maeve said.

Changing the subject, Dad asked her, "What year are you in at UNCW?"

"I'm a senior with a double major in Education and English."

Knowing she wouldn't volunteer the information, I added, "Maeve was accepted at Yale, but she liked UNCW better."

Maeve gave me a menacing look, but noting my mother's interested expression, explained.

"I actually spent one year at Yale. Didn't really like it. It wasn't the school itself so much as the weather. Winter came too early and got too cold."

"I know what you mean, dear," my mom said. "I would not move back up north for anything. I have loved it here since Owen first brought me home, and I have no intention of leaving."

Malori added her opinion. "UNCW is okay, but I think I'd like to go to Appalachian, or maybe State up in Raleigh. Chapel Hill is just too, I don't know, too something for me."

"Malori, you'll wind up at Harvard or Yale the way you're going," Dad said.

"I'd rather go to Cape Fear Tech," Malori said, looking horrified at the idea.

"Malori, we do not have to decide that right now. Please concentrate on keeping us off the shoals," my mom said.

No sooner had the words left my mother's mouth than Malori pulled the wheel hard to port.

CHAPTER TEN

October 1983

Words escaped Malori's mouth that should never be uttered by an eleven-year-old. "Who anchors a dinghy in the middle of the channel and just leaves it there?" she yelled into the dark.

She turned the wheel back to starboard and pulled the throttle to neutral. The boat, which hadn't been moving that fast, rocked back and forth as it drifted slowly past the dark green johnboat we'd nearly collided with.

"I don't think it's anchored," Dad said, his voice shaky from the near miss. "I don't see any lines on it. It probably wasn't pulled ashore far enough, and floated off when the tide came in."

"Either way," Mom chimed in, unflappable even in those circumstances, "we cannot just leave it floating around the sound."

"You're right, dear," Dad replied. "Malori, come

about and bring us alongside. Michael, grab a boathook and get hold of it. We'll beach it here, and the owner can find it in the morning."

"Should we let the Coast Guard know about it?" I asked as I dug the boat hook out of the storage locker.

"I will take care of that," my mom said, picking up the mike on Dad's Marine VHF Radio.

Once we'd beached the johnboat, which required Malori and me to get our feet wet, and notified the Coast Guard in case someone reported the missing boat to them, we continued our cruise north up the sound and under the Highway 76 Bridge. The thrum of our motor was the only noise on the dark water.

Few lights pierced the night on the sound side of Wrightsville Beach. On a late fall Sunday night, there weren't many businesses open. The lights of one reflecting on the calm waters of the sound caught my father's eye.

"Look, Giuseppe's is open," he called out. "Who's in the mood for ice cream?"

"Me, me, I am!" Malori said.

"I think that sounds like a wonderful idea. Maeve, what do you think?" Mom asked.

"Eunice, I'd love some ice cream." Maeve turned her blue eyes on me and smiled. "Michael?"

With a laugh, I told her, "I never say no to Giuseppe's Ice Cream."

Giuseppe made all his own ice cream there at the shop. It was the richest, smoothest, best tasting ice cream I've ever had. Giuseppe had a few standard flavors: vanilla, chocolate, strawberry; and that night he had one of my favorites, fudge caramel swirl. I once suggested he make ice cream with chocolate chip cookie dough. He said no one would like that; it would never sell.

"I am so glad to see you have pistachio." My mother said, smiling at the young lady working at the ice cream counter. Her name tag said, "Ann." "Pistachio is my favorite. I would like a double scoop in a sugar cone, please."

When it was my father's turn, he ordered a double scoop of chocolate in a plain cone.

"Giuseppe's chocolate is so good, I don't know why you guys get anything else."

"You guys don't have any raspberry splash?" Malori asked, clearly disappointed she didn't see any in the ice cream case. Ann shook her head.

Malori sighed dramatically. "I guess I'll have strawberry then."

Ann slid open the freezer, then stopped. "What kind of cone would you like?"

Malori pursed her lips and looked back and forth between the sugar and plain cones.

"Oh, for Pete's sake," I said. "Just pick one, Malori."

Malori turned and stuck her tongue out at me. "Don't rush me."

Maeve chuckled. Malori gave her a wink and turned back to Ann.

"I'll have a double scoop on a sugar cone, please."

Ann smiled and said, "Comin' right up."

Maeve went next, pleased her favorite was there.

"I'd like a single scoop of mint chocolate chip in a

cup, please."

Ann reached around and grabbed a small Styrofoam bowl from the counter behind her.

"Just one scoop?" she asked, holding up the bowl for Maeve.

Maeve looked at me.

"You know you want a double," I teased.

Maeve laughed, and then told Ann, "Okay, make it two."

Ann nodded and smiled, filling Maeve's bowl with two scoops of green ice cream."

Maeve took her bowl and joined the others out on the dock. It suddenly occurred to me I'd be buying everyone's ice cream. I laughed and shook my head.

"Looks like they stuck you with the bill," Ann observed. "Night out with the family?"

Still chuckling, I nodded. "I shoulda seen it coming."

"Nice family. Your sisters are cute."

Something in her tone and the look in her eyes caught my attention. It was the way she said 'sisters' in a hopeful way. I licked my lips and gently corrected her.

"The little one's my sister. The other one's my girlfriend."

Ann's lips twisted into a wry smile.

"Figures. Too bad, you're kinda cute."

Her compliment made me feel self-conscious. I looked down at my hands and mumbled, "Thanks."

"S'okay. Do you want some ice cream?"

I ordered a single scoop of fudge caramel swirl on a

sugar cone and paid the tab, adding a generous tip for Ann.

Having gotten our fill of ice cream, we continued up the sound towards the Wright Island Junior Mariner Camp. The camp was established through my trust to provide opportunities for disadvantaged kids to learn sailing and seamanship. Operated by a partnership of the Scouts, the Boys Club, and the YMCA, it was located on an island at the north end of the sound just beyond the Highway 74 bridge. Circling round the island, we headed south down the sound towards my folks' place. Arriving at their dock, we disembarked, tied off, and said our goodbyes.

"We really need to be heading back to town," I said. "As late as it is, I don't know how I'll drag myself out of bed to my first class tomorrow."

"My first class is early, too," Maeve told them. "I've had a wonderful time. Thank you for having me over."

"It's been our pleasure. You're welcome in our home anytime, Maeve," my father said as they walked us to the car.

"Yes, anytime. We will be setting a place for you at our table on Sundays, Maeve. Next week we will make sure to leave time for some piano," Mom said.

Maeve smiled and hugged her. "Absolutely, Eunice. I look forward to it."

"I'll see you next week, Maeve. I suppose you can bring my brother if you want," Malori said when she hugged Maeve.

That got a chuckle out of Maeve. "I might do that. I've gotten quite attached to him, you know."

"Good night, you two, drive safely," Mom said.

Malori gave me a nod and went into the house. Mom hugged me and then followed her.

Dad stepped up and hugged Maeve. "Maeve, it's been a pleasure. I hope we'll be seeing a lot more of you."

"I hope so too, Mr. Lanier," Maeve said.

"It's Owen, please."

"Thank you, Owen. Good night." She gave him another quick hug before he went inside.

We climbed into the car, and Maeve said, "You have a very nice family."

"They're not my real family," I said. "I rented them for the night to make a good impression on you."

Maeve rolled her eyes and gave me a sharp look. "Your mother's right. You can be a brat sometimes."

With an astonished look, I replied, "She said that about sweet lovable me?"

"Hmmm," was Maeve's response.

As we turned left onto the Highway 76 Bridge, Maeve made an interesting observation.

"Mike, you know, now that I've been to dinner with your parents, on such short notice I might add, you're kind of obligated to marry me."

"Okay," I replied.

"Okay?" she asked.

"Yes," I said.

Looking hard at me, she said, "You're serious, aren't you?"

"Yes," I said.

Sitting back in her seat, Maeve took a deep breath.

"Wow, all this happened so fast."

Smiling, I asked her, "Are you having second thoughts?"

"Am I having second thoughts about what?" Maeve asked, a bit confused.

"Are you having second thoughts about marrying me?"

"As a matter of fact, no. I decided I wanted to marry you Friday night on the front porch at River Dream. I was just wondering how to get you to realize you needed to ask me."

"For the record, you asked me," I said.

"I didn't really ask you. I asked you if you understood that you needed to ask me."

Without so much as a turn signal, I braked hard and pulled into the Wildlife Boat Ramp parking lot as the drawbridge. After taking a small box out of the glove compartment, I got out and walked around to her side of the car. I opened her door, helped her out, and led her to the end of the dock.

"Uh, Mike, what are we doing?" Maeve asked.

I gestured for her to sit on the bench at the end of the dock. Carefully, I got down on one knee and began.

"Maeve, I don't know how long it takes to fall in love. I do know I'm in love with you. Now, when I look into my soul, where I used to see one light burning, there are two. The other light is you. Yours is the soul that completes mine. I cannot see a future for me that does not include you by my side for the rest of my days. Maeve, I love you. I want you to be with me in everything I do, everywhere I go. You are my soulmate, my life's partner."

I opened the little box with the engagement ring I'd been carrying around all weekend and held it out to her. "Maeve, I want you to be my wife. Will you marry me?"

Maeve reached out and gently touched my face. Tears filled her eyes. I offered a silent prayer they were happy tears.

"Oh, Michael, my darling Michael. Yes, I'll marry you. For so long, I could only dream of ever finding you again. Now you're here, and you love me the way I have loved you for so long. Yes, Michael, I'll marry you."

Taking the ring from the box, I placed it on her finger. Rising slowly to sit on the bench next to her, I took her in my arms, and we sealed our promise with a kiss. I don't know how long we would have stayed there if -

"Are you kids going to fish or waste this tide kissing?" the old gentleman asked.

Embarrassed that we suddenly had an audience, we apologized to the gentleman, got to our feet, and started towards the car.

"No need to apologize to me, young fellow. I might be well past my prime, but I haven't forgotten what it was like."

Unable to contain myself, I had to tell him. "Sir, she just said she'd marry me."

"Well then, congratulations. Odd place to propose, I suppose, but anyway, congratulations."

Maeve and I finally made it to her apartment. Kim

was already asleep. A big yawn escaped me as we walked through the door.

Maeve looked at me with concern in her eyes. She reached up and gently touched my cheek.

"Why don't you spend the night? Our couch folds down into a bed, of sorts."

I thought about it for a moment. Their couch didn't look promising. "It's not that far back to the dorm."

"No," Maeve said, "but considering how early we were up, and everything you've done today, I'd feel better if you stayed here tonight. That way I don't have to worry about you getting back to the dorm in one piece."

Since it seemed so important to her, I gave in. "You don't think Kim will mind?"

Realizing she'd won, Maeve shook her head. "Kim will be okay with it, especially since we're engaged now." With a coy smile she added, "In fact, Kim's hinted that she's surprised you haven't spent the night before now."

Reaching up to pull a blanket and pillow from the closet, I asked, "And what did you tell her?"

"I told her you probably would have, but the single beds in our rooms are too small, and you didn't want to sleep on the floor. And that you sleep naked and often kick your covers off in the night, so didn't want to sleep on the couch."

"You did not tell her that."

Maeve took the blanket and pillow from me, leaving me to figure out how the couch converted to a bed. Figuring it out didn't take long. There was a tag sewn onto the back with instructions.

"Okay. I didn't tell her about the naked part." She pointed a finger at me. "You're not going to tonight, are you? Not on the couch."

I shrugged and started unbuckling my belt.

Maeve slapped me on the shoulder. "Don't you dare."

"Just gonna take off my belt," I said. "And my shoes. Everything else stays on."

Satisfied I would behave myself, Maeve put the blanket and pillow on the couch, which was now my bed, and turned and put her arms around me.

"Goodnight, fiancé. Sleep tight."

I hugged her close and kissed her gently. "Goodnight, future Mrs. Lanier. I love you."

Maeve smiled and laid her head against my chest. "Maeve Lanier. I like the sound of that. I love you, Michael."

She kissed me once more before heading down the hall to her bedroom. I tried to get comfortable on the couch. Thanks to the lateness of the hour and the busy day we'd had, I fell right asleep.

CHAPTER ELEVEN

October 1983

From somewhere far away, an annoying buzzing began invading my sleep. I knew it couldn't be time to get up. My head had barely hit the pillow.

I opened one eye just a sliver. It didn't look like my dorm room. For a minute, I couldn't figure out where I was. With effort, I opened my other eye.

With a start, I realized I was in Maeve's apartment, on Maeve's couch. Maeve - the woman I asked to be my wife.

Abruptly, the alarm stopped sounding. Looking sleepy in her bathrobe and slippers, Maeve walked into the living room.

"Good morning, the future Mrs. Lanier," I said, repeating my words from the night before. Rolling my shoulders to work the kinks out of my back, I sat up and tried to stifle a groan.

"Good morning, future husband of mine," Maeve

said. She motioned for me to make room for her on the couch and sat down beside me. "I suppose you have to get up and get going."

"Yeah, I guess I should. So should you, for that matter."

Maeve glanced at the clock and asked, "Do you have time for a cup of coffee before you leave?"

Pondering how long it would take me to get to the dorm, shower and change, and get to class, I figured I could just make it.

"I think so. But I'd better call Derrick. He'll be wondering where I've been all night. He'll also want to know if I worked up the nerve to pop the question."

"Yes, you'd better do that then," Maeve said, getting up to make the coffee. As the last thing I'd said sank in, she turned back. "Wait a minute. Derrick knew about the ring?"

"Well, yeah. He helped me pick it out. After Kim told me what kind of stone you'd like."

"Kim was in on this, too?" Maeve asked, straightening up and putting her hands on her hips.

I couldn't help but laugh. "She didn't know I'd bought the ring. Just that I was asking casually what kind of ring you might like."

"And she never said a thing. You are both brats. All three of you are brats." Maeve laughed as she walked into the kitchen.

I called Derrick and filled him in on why I hadn't made it back to the dorm the night before. While I was talking to him, Kim came out of her room.

"Well, good morning, That Mike. You're here

rather early." Her surprise at seeing me was clear on her face.

"Actually, he's here rather late," Maeve called out from the kitchen. "My fiancé spent the night on the couch."

Kim's eyes widened at the announcement. "Your fiancé spent the night? That must have been some dinner with the folks."

Maeve came back into the living room. "Dinner was great. On the way home, Mike picked a romantic, secluded, waterside spot to pop the question."

"Whatdaya know about that? Congrats, you two. So, how soon do I have to start looking for a new roommate? Or is Mike moving in with us?"

"We haven't gotten that far yet," I said.

"No, I don't suppose you've had time to set a date or anything. Well, I'm cool with you moving in here for a while," Kim said.

Maeve and I glanced at each other. I could tell she didn't think that was a good idea any more than I did.

"I'm sure we'll get something worked out soon, won't we, Mike?" Maeve said before going back in the kitchen to check on the coffee.

I got up off the couch and said, "I'm sure we will, but not right now. I've really gotta get going."

"Okay, coffee's ready. Take a cup with you." Maeve rooted around in the cabinet until she found a travel mug.

Gingerly holding the mug, I gave Maeve a kiss. "Thanks, babe. Bye, I love you."

Maeve took my face in her hands and pulled me

towards her for another kiss. "I love you, too. I'll call as soon as I get home."

"Okay, bye," I said, and walked out the door.

"Bye," Maeve said.

"Aren't you going to tell me goodbye?" Kim asked, hands on her hips.

"Goodbye, Kim," I said with a bow, being very careful not to spill my coffee.

"Bye bye," I heard her say before she started laughing.

I hurried back to the dorm, grabbed a quick shower, dressed, and made it to class with only minutes to spare.

Since I hadn't cracked a book all weekend, I was glad the next assignment for English wasn't due until Wednesday. There was Statistics homework due, but I could finish it at breakfast.

I didn't see Derrick until lunch that afternoon. It turned out he'd grabbed an early breakfast because he had an interview.

As we sat down, I asked him, "What kind of interview?"

"The job kind," Derrick replied, looking at me like he thought it was a dumb question.

He reached for the ketchup and poured a generous helping onto his fries.

Realizing I should have worded the question better, I rephrased. "What kind of job did you interview for?"

"It's a part-time gig at the martial arts studio." Derrick was a martial arts master and a certified instructor. "I heard they had a position for an instructor. I'd teach one class a night, and a couple on Saturdays. I'll only be working seven or eight hours a week, but it pays ten dollars an hour. Easy money, man."

Stopping halfway to getting the cover off my barbeque sauce, I looked up and asked, "Won't that cut into your study time?"

Derrick worked hard to keep his grades up. Maybe I was feeling a little big brotherly, but I didn't want to see a job mess that up for him.

"Not much, but, dude," he looked at me sheepishly, "it will cut back on our workouts some."

I smiled and shook my head. "Because you'll use that time for schoolwork since you'll be getting your workouts at the studio."

He took that as acceptance. "Yeah, thanks for understanding, man."

"All right. But if it doesn't work out, I may have something for you. If you're game."

Derrick had never mentioned wanting a job. If he had, I certainly could have helped him find something that would fit his study schedule.

"Something like what, Mike?"

"Let's just wait to see if you get this job or not, okay, Derrick?"

Nodding, he said, "You are a sneaky dude sometimes, Michael. Alright, we'll wait and see."

Changing the subject, he asked, "So, did you pop the question? Where and how?"

"It was last night, on the way back from my folks.

It was a perfect evening. My family loved her. Within minutes, it was as if she'd belonged there all along. I'm telling you it was kismet." I sat back and smiled as I remembered.

Derrick swallowed the last bite of his cheeseburger. "So, on the way home, you popped the question. Where?"

"At the Wildlife Ramp by the drawbridge. I walked her out to the end of the dock, got down on one knee and proposed."

"Dude, you asked her to marry you at the Wildlife Ramp?"

Hearing him say it, it didn't sound nearly as romantic as it had been.

"It was a spur-of-the-moment decision. We were talking about getting married, and I was suddenly moved to just do it. I know it doesn't sound like it, but with the lights reflecting on the water and all, it was kind of romantic."

"If you say so, man. At least you know she'll never forget how, or where, you proposed."

He glanced at the clock over the door. "I've got to get going. Will you be staying in the dorm tonight?"

"I imagine so. Maeve's couch isn't very comfortable. I'll let you know."

After classes and working out with Derrick at the gym, I went back to the dorm to study and wait for Maeve's call. Late afternoon was quiet in the dorm. I'd almost fallen asleep at my desk when the phone rang.

"Hi, babe, I'm just leaving the bookstore on my way to class. I'll just have time to swing by the apartment to grab my books. Can you meet me there and walk me to class?"

Maeve had a night class on Monday and Wednesday nights, a curse of her double major.

"Sure, I can do that. Will you have time to grab a bite?"

After a short pause, she said, "Not before class. Maybe before we go to the library."

"Remind me what time you get out of class?"

"We usually finish up by seven-thirty," Maeve said. "Can you meet me then?"

"I can and I will, my love," I assured her with a dramatic flair. With her mind already on other things, she didn't catch it.

"Okay, Mike. See you at the apartment shortly."

I noticed she didn't say "my apartment," rather "the apartment." Did that mean anything? She always called it "my apartment" before. Either way, I hurried over there. Just in case, I threw my overnight bag into the trunk of my GTO. I'd just parked when Maeve pulled up.

"You're right on time," she said with a smile, coming over to give me a kiss.

"I didn't want to miss one second with you by being late," I said as I put my arms around her.

"What a sweet thing to say. Just for that, I'll let you carry my books to class."

We were in the apartment only long enough for her to stuff her notebook into her already overfilled tote bag and hand me her textbook. It was hefty. It was then that I realized I'd left my books and notes in my dorm room. I'd just have to make an extra trip to pick them up after I dropped Maeve off at class. She gave me a quick kiss when we got to her class.

I hoofed it back to the dorm, picked up my things, and got over to the library with enough time to get a little work done before I had to meet Maeve.

Later, when she saw me waiting outside her building, Maeve grinned and said, "You had to run back to your dorm and pick up your books, didn't you?"

Caught, I confessed. "Yeah, I did. How did you know?"

"You didn't have them when we walked over here from the apartment," she said with a satisfied smile.

"You're a regular Nancy Drew, aren't you?" I said while holding the door open for her.

"No, but I did read all her books."

We walked down the steps and headed for the Seahawks' Nest.

"Really, I read all the Hardy Boys. I always wanted to be as smart as Frank and as cool as Joe. I wound up more like Chet."

With a coy smile, she said, "Oh, I wouldn't say that."

She gave me a kiss on the cheek, giggled, and sprang her trap. "Chet was way more cool than you."

"And you call me a brat," I said to her back as she scampered away. I caught up at the door to the Nest.

We went through the line and ordered our food. Sitting down at a table, Maeve gestured at the food on her tray.

"The food here's a lot better than it was when I first came here last year."

"Probably because they've got a real catering company making the food now."

Maeve set her sandwich down and looked up at me. "And how would you know that?"

"My dad told me the college hired a new company over the summer. One run by the lady that used to manage the Bonanza Steakhouse on Market Street."

Maeve interrupted, "Don't tell me. Let me finish the story. You learned about it, or knew her somehow, and arranged for the financing she needed to go out on her own."

"I may have had a hand in getting the ball rolling for her," I said.

"I think it's great what you do for folks around here," Maeve said. "And they don't know it's you?"

"I like to keep it that way. Besides, it's not all altruism. Over 90% have turned out to be good investments."

Maeve leaned over the table and gave me a kiss.

"All the same, I think it's wonderful what you do. It's just one more thing for me to love about you. Now, if you're done with your supper, let's go to the library and get to work."

I gulped down the last of my fries. We cleaned our table, picked up our books, and headed to the library.

CHAPTER TWELVE

October 1983

When we got to the apartment, Kim was already there, and very upset.

"Kim, what's the matter?" Maeve asked, moving to sit beside her friend on the couch.

"It's that idiot boyfriend of mine. Or should I say, ex-boyfriend. There I am at work, and the jerk comes into my restaurant with another woman. What an idiot. What a jerk."

Kim's makeup was streaked from the tears she'd been crying.

"I can't believe he'd do that to you," Maeve said, putting her arm around Kim's shoulder.

Kim leaned against Maeve. "Well, he did. I wanted to cuss him out right then and there, but I didn't. I would have lost my job. I guess he was too gutless to tell me he wanted to break up. He decided to show me instead."

"Kimmy, I'm so sorry. Is there anything I can do?" Maeve asked.

"Not unless you know someone who could teach him a good lesson for me," Kim said. The anger in her voice left no doubt as to the lesson she wanted to see taught.

Maeve gave me a cautionary look. "No, I can't do that."

I could, but I went along with Maeve and didn't bring that up. Instead, I suggested it was time for me to go.

Kim gave me a funny look. "Go where, That Mike? This is your place now, too, you know. I'm not going to run you off."

Kim tried to smile. Maeve gave me a 'don't argue and I'll explain it later' look.

"Okay, Kim. Thanks."

Not knowing what else to do, I sat down in the easy chair.

Kim laughed a weak laugh. "Hmm, Maeve, he's friendly and courteous. He must have been a Boy Scout."

I was an Eagle Scout, but again, not the time to bring that up.

"I don't know about that," Maeve said. "But I'm glad you're not making me send him back to the dorm. I mean, if you want me to, I will."

Kim shook her head emphatically. "No, I want him to stay. It's nice to have someone around to remind me that not all men are jerks."

Maeve suggested I get some ice cream out of the

freezer. That surprised me. I expected they'd open a bottle of wine or something.

"I don't touch the stuff," Kim said. "My mom was an alcoholic. That's why my dad took us kids and left her in Oregon. He moved us clear over here to NC to keep us as far away from her as possible. I hated him for it for a while. Later, I understood why he'd done it."

I could certainly understand how she felt. "I don't drink either. My dad's brother was killed by a drunk driver when I was little. I decided then and there I wouldn't touch the stuff."

"Right now, Kim needs a big bowl of chocolate ice cream, swimming in chocolate syrup and covered with chocolate sprinkles," Maeve said.

"Thanks so much, guys," Kim said, looking from one of us to the other. "I feel better already."

After indulging in a bowl of chocolate therapy, Kim announced she was ready to go to bed. Maeve looked at me and tilted her head toward the kitchen. Taking the hint, I took the bowls to the kitchen and washed them out while the ladies had a private moment. Then, Kim went to her room, and Maeve joined me in the kitchen.

Looking down the hall toward her friend's room, Maeve said, "That was kind of a bummer."

I put my arms around her and pulled her close. "She's lucky to have a good friend like you."

Maeve laid her head on my chest. "I always knew that guy was no good for her."

"Now she'll be free to find someone new," I said, "someone she deserves."

"I hope so. I hope she finds a man as wonderful as mine."

Maeve wrapped her arms more tightly around me. We stayed that way for a while, and then she led me back to the living room.

"I hate making you sleep on the couch, but it's either there or the dorm unless you want us both to try to squeeze onto my bed."

"I don't want to leave, but your couch is not conducive to a good night's sleep, and if we try to share your bed, neither of us would sleep well."

She laughed. "Do you have to leave right away?"

I probably should have, but I really didn't want to. "I can stay a little longer."

We sat together on the couch. Snuggling into my shoulder, she asked, "Do you know a lady named Sara Tomlinson?"

I had to think for a minute. "My Spanish teacher at Laney High was Miss Tomlinson. I think her first name was Sara. Why?"

"You know my night class," Maeve said. "It's a combined class of undergrads and grad students. Sara's in my class."

Wondering why she thought I'd be interested, I said, "I guess it could be the same person."

Maeve's eyes sparkled with mischief. "I think so. She knows you. She asked about you."

Now I was truly puzzled. "What did she want to know?"

"She saw us together in the library," Maeve said. "Then in class, she asked me how I knew you."

"Why didn't she just come over and say hi?" I asked.

Maeve shrugged. "I don't know. I told her we were dating. Tonight, she noticed the ring and asked if it was from you. I told her you proposed. She sends her congratulations, by the way."

While Maeve talked, I was remembering Miss Tomlinson. I smiled, recalling the time before homeroom when my girlfriend Jill surprised me with a kiss outside Miss Tomlinson's door. My smile grew as I remembered another day during senior year.

Miss Tomlinson was working late and needed a ride home. Being the gallant gentleman I was, I gave her a ride in my GTO after soccer practice. I put the top down and can still picture the wind blowing through her hair as we cruised down South College Road. I had a bit of a crush on her. I decided Maeve didn't need to know that.

"Did you know she lives right here in University Arms?" Maeve asked.

I should have thought before I answered. "If I remember right, she lives one building over, two doors down."

Maeve sat up and looked at me through narrowed eyes. "Just how would you know that?"

It was time for damage control. "In high school, after soccer practice one day, Miss Tomlinson needed a ride. I offered to take her home. That's all there was to it."

Maeve pursed her lips and thought that over. Satisfied there was nothing more to it, she settled back against my shoulder.

"Anyway, she said she wished she had the money to buy her friend's house. Someone named Jenny Nadeau. I guess her friend is moving soon."

"I remember Mrs. Nadeau. She taught French at Laney. Where's she moving to?"

Then I had another thought; the Nadeaus lived at the beach.

Maeve turned and gave me an irritated look. "Do you remember any of your male teachers?"

I pretended to give it some thought. "Now that you mention it, no."

That earned me an elbow to the gut.

"Sara said something about Jenny moving to Charleston," Maeve said, followed by a big yawn.

"So, you and Sara have become pretty good friends?" I asked.

The only response I got was her rhythmic breathing. She'd fallen asleep. It didn't look like I was going to make it back to the dorm. Pulling the blanket off the back of the couch, I spread it over us and tried to get comfortable. As I fell asleep, a plan formed.

CHAPTER THIRTEEN

October 1983

On October 25, 1983, US Forces, along with those of several Caribbean nations, invaded the island of Grenada to reverse a communist coup led by Castro-supported and backed members of the Grenadian military. It wasn't easy for me watching it unfold on television, knowing that had things been different, I would've deployed with the small boat units delivering SEAL Teams to the beaches.

None of my friends in Wilmington - not even Maeve - really knew what I'd done in the Navy. They just knew what I'd told them; I'd been a boat driver. That had been fine with me before, but I could tell Maeve was concerned with how I was reacting to the news of the invasion.

Seeing the worried look on her face, I tried to

explain. "Honey, I'm just feeling ... I don't know ... like I'm missing out on something, like I'm letting our side down somehow."

"But Mike, you did your service. Besides, what would you be doing if you were there? You'd just be at the helm of one of the ships, right?"

It was time to give Maeve a better idea of what I'd done in the Navy.

"Not exactly, sweetheart," I said. "Actually, I'd probably be crewing one of those small boats putting SEALs on the beach."

Maeve's eyes widened with surprise. "That's the kind of boats you drove? I thought you were just being facetious when you said you drove boats. I figured you meant you were a helmsman on a ship or something."

"Well, no, I didn't really spend much time on board ship unless we were being transported somewhere." I felt a stab of regret I hadn't told her more, sooner.

"You were some kind of SEAL?" Maeve asked.

"No, honey, we were called Boat Men."

"Oh, that's a funny name," Maeve said.

"Yeah," I said, "I guess so."

Maeve didn't ask me anything more about it after that. I was glad, because I wasn't ready to talk much more about it. I was proud to have served my country, but there were some things I still couldn't talk about with people who hadn't been there.

CHAPTER FOURTEEN

November 1983

Sleeping on Maeve's couch became the norm for me over the next couple of weeks. It didn't get any more comfortable, but I got used to it. I thought Kim might tire of my being around, but she assured me I was welcome.

The week after Maeve told me about meeting Sara Tomlinson, I asked my dad to look into whether the Nadeau's house was on the market. It wasn't yet, so I asked the people at Coastal Carolina Realty Trust to offer them a premium price for their place. I made sure my folks didn't say anything to Maeve. I wanted to surprise her.

The staff at CCRT let me know that Mr. Nadeau thought the offer was fair, but he wanted time to think about it. I suspected he was checking around to be sure it was a good deal. Evidently, he learned he couldn't expect a better offer. They accepted.

On the Friday after our trip to River Dream, Maeve and I stayed in town and went to a Laney High football game. Sara had game duty, and she talked Maeve into bringing me. At the game, a few of my old teachers came up and congratulated us on our engagement. So did Mr. McHale, who was *still* the principal. The Buccaneers won a nail biter, scoring a field goal with thirty seconds left to secure the victory.

On Saturday, it was my turn to visit Maeve's parents. Before backing my GTO out of the parking spot in front of Maeve's apartment, I asked the question that had worried me for days. "Do you think they'll be ticked we got engaged before I met them?"

Maeve tilted her head and squinted at me. "It's not like they've never met you, Michael. They remember seeing you at Camp."

Her reply did little to ease my worry. "Yeah, but only once or twice, for, like, two minutes. They don't really know me."

Softly, Maeve said, "They know more about you than you think."

We were stopped at the light, waiting for it to turn green so we could turn onto South College Road.

"What does that mean?"

"Nothing bad, Michael. There's something I haven't told you."

Judging by her expression, she was wrestling with how to say what she wanted to tell me.

The light turned green. Maeve waited until I'd

made it through the gears to continue. "After that summer we spent together, you know, when you brought *Riverscape* home?"

She made it a question and looked at me until I nodded. "I remember."

"When I got home, I broke up with Roger."

I let that news digest for a moment before I asked, "Why?"

Maeve took a deep breath and let it out slowly before answering my question with one of her own. "Why do you think?

Glancing at her out of the corner of my eye, I saw she was looking at her hands in her lap. We stopped at a red light. I turned my head to look at her. She kept staring at her hands, fingers gently brushing her engagement ring.

"Because of me?"

Maeve smiled and looked up at me. Her blue eyes sparkled. "Because of you, Michael. I was in love with you. There was no way things could work between Roger and me. I couldn't stop thinking about you."

She'd hinted at this before, the night we'd first admitted our feelings for each other. But I never knew, hoped maybe, but never knew she'd been in love with me back then.

"Why didn't you tell me? Why didn't you let me know?"

Maeve shrugged. "We'd both agreed that our ... friendship ... our summer love affair was just a summer thing."

"It was supposed to be over when summer was

over. I went home to Roger and my life. You went back to Jill and Rhiannon and your life. I'd made it plain I wasn't looking for anything more, and so had you."

I couldn't argue with her. We'd both felt exactly that way at the start. By the end of summer, maybe not so much.

Getting back to how we'd gotten on this subject, Maeve said, "Anyway, my mom wanted to know why I suddenly broke up with Roger. So, I told her about you. Thinking you'd meant what you said about not wanting something more, I tried to forget you." She sighed. "That didn't work out."

Maeve reached toward the gearshift and put her hand over mine. "Then, when I saw you in the library - well, as they say - the rest is history. Or in this case," she smiled, "our story."

I returned her smile. "What have you told your folks about the latest chapter in 'our story'?"

Maeve laughed, reached up, and gently stroked my cheek. "Everything."

"Everything?"

"Well, almost everything." She raised her eyebrows, tucked her head towards her shoulder, and grinned.

My stomach had tightened into a lead ball by the time we pulled onto her parents' street in Whiteville. Images of her father waiting on the porch with a shotgun, prepared to send me on my way with a trunk full of buckshot, paraded through my too-fertile imagination.

Maeve, in contrast, was all bright smiles and

shining eyes, rocking back and forth in her seat as we got closer.

"That's it, Michael. See the Salt-and-Pepper brick house, the one with the - there's my dad on the porch."

She rolled down her window and waved as we pulled into the driveway. "Hi, Daddy. We're here. We made it."

Her father wasn't toting a shotgun. He didn't look like he was ready to run me off. Mr. Dalton waved back at his daughter and, beaming a smile, walked down the brick path across the front yard to meet us in the driveway. That lead ball in my gut began to dissolve.

"I can see that, sweetheart," he called out as he got closer. "And right on time, too. Dinner's just about ready."

I'd barely gotten out the door when Mr. Dalton grabbed my hand in his. "It's good to see you again, Mike. It's been a long time."

Recovering quickly, I returned his firm grip pound-for-pound, while being careful not to outdo him. "Yes, sir. Not since Camp Riversail back when."

His attention quickly turned to Maeve as she came around the car. He dropped my hand and held out his arms to his daughter. "Come give your father a hug, young lady."

Things went better than I expected. Maeve seemed pleased with how well her father, Ted, and I got along. Her mother was very sweet. Phyllis had already decided that if I made her daughter happy, I was okay in her book. By the time Ted walked us to the car, after a delicious dessert of homemade apple pie a la mode, my worries about Maeve's folks resenting me were gone.

Maeve's older sister worried me, though. Cynthia seemed rather taciturn and didn't warm up to me much. In a private moment in the kitchen, I'd told Maeve, "I get the feeling your sister doesn't like me much."

Maeve had looked up from the sink, her lips twisted into a puzzled frown. "What makes you say that? Cynthia's exact words to me were, 'You did alright, kid. He seems like a decent guy.' Coming from my sister, that's high praise."

CHAPTER FIFTEEN

November 1983

On a Monday night, on our way home from the library, I told Maeve I thought we should get married.

Maeve looked at me like I'd lost my marbles. "Babe, we have decided to get married, remember? You proposed, and I said yes."

"What I mean is, I think we should get married now," I said. "After all, we're practically living together."

Things had gotten to the point where I was more or less living in her apartment, even if I was sleeping on the couch. Most nights we wound up sleeping on the couch together. It made for a slighter wider bed than she had in her bedroom.

"In almost every way, we're living and acting like a married couple. Let's make it official."

Maeve tilted her head and squinted at me. "How can we just throw a wedding together on such short notice? Those things take time to plan, you know?"

Obviously, I wasn't making myself clear. "I'm not saying we have a wedding right now. I'm saying we go see a magistrate and get married. Next spring we'd still have a big event and invite all our family and friends."

"But if we're already married, why would they come to the wedding?" Maeve asked. It was a perfectly reasonable question.

"Mostly for the free food, I imagine," I said, thinking it was a perfectly reasonable answer.

"Brat!" Maeve said.

Clearly, I'd not won her over. "No, really, I think they'll come. They'll want to come. We'll invite them to come see us repeat our vows before God, family, and friends. They'll come to celebrate our love and our new life together. Mostly, they'll come for a couple of days at the beach."

We reached the apartment and were standing at the door.

"You really are a brat, but I love you anyway. Okay, maybe they will still come," Maeve said. "So how do we go about getting married?"

I knew then she'd decided we should do it. Having already looked into it, I said, "Tomorrow, we go down to the Registrar of Deeds office with a couple of witnesses, get a marriage license, and get married."

I unlocked the door, and we went inside.

Setting her books down on the coffee table, Maeve turned to me and said, "Just like that, we go down there and tie the knot. Anxious fiancé of mine, do you think we could wait until Friday? I would like to at least let our parents know what we're doing. Who do you plan to take along as witnesses?"

"I thought I'd ask Derrick, and you could ask Kim. But if we're going to wait all the way until Friday, I'll see if Hans can make it down from Raleigh."

Maeve smiled at my impatience. "Friday will be here before you know it, Mike. I'll call Cynthia and see if she can come down. We can still ask Derrick and Kim to come, either way. They are right here after all."

"I wonder how many people will fit in that office," I said, making a big show of stroking my chin thoughtfully.

"What makes you say that?" Maeve asked.

"Well, you've got three days to see how many people you can get here by Friday afternoon. The Register of Deeds may need a bigger office."

"You brat! Just for that, you can go sleep in the dorm tonight."

Serious for a moment, I said, "Maybe that wouldn't be a bad idea."

"What!?" Maeve said.

"If we're going to make it official on Friday, maybe I should stay in the dorm until then."

Maeve grabbed my arm and turned me to face her.

"Buster, if you think I'm gonna let you cruise on back to that dorm for some last-minute partying with your buddies, you are officially out of your mind." Then she pulled me close and kissed me hard.

Tuesday morning, I should have been able to sleep in. My English professor was away at some sort of conference. He'd left us a big writing assignment to work on while he was gone. He wouldn't get back until the following Tuesday.

Maeve wasn't so lucky. She still had to get up and go to class. I didn't lounge around, though. I got up, made her breakfast, and headed for the gym to meet Derrick. I wanted to let him know what was in the works for Friday.

Derrick was finishing his workout when I arrived. We walked to the Nest to get some breakfast. He listened carefully while I told him what Maeve and I had planned.

Once I finished, he was quiet for a moment before saying, "Let me see if I understand this. You're going to get married on Friday but have the wedding next spring."

"Yes, that's the gist of it," I said, pulling open the door to the Nest and gesturing for him to go first.

He sounded anything but convinced it was a good idea. "I never heard of anyone doing that before. Don't most people wait and get married at their wedding?"

"I believe that's the traditional way it's done," I said. "Doesn't mean it always has to be that way. C'mon, these are the 80s. The times they are a changing."

Derrick nodded. "How's this going to work? You just go downtown, get a license, and that's that?"

"We go down to the Register of Deeds to get the license, and then see a magistrate to perform the service," I said. Then it was our turn to order.

While we were waiting for our food, Derrick

continued, "That sounds easy enough. Then what happens?"

"Maeve and I fly up to River Dream. We're supposed to work Family Sailing Weekend."

Derrick frowned and said, "Doesn't sound like much of a honeymoon."

"I guess not. Our real honeymoon comes next summer, after the wedding." Pressing the point home, I asked, "Derrick, could you come downtown with us Friday as a witness for the ceremony?"

He brightened at that. "Sure I would."

In the interest of full disclosure, I told him, "I'm going to call my friend Hans to see if he can come, too. I'd like you both there."

"Dude, I'll be there," Derrick said.

Later in the day, I called Hans. Once I convinced him I was serious, he said he'd definitely be coming.

Maeve called Cynthia, who, after getting over the shock, said she'd come. That evening we both talked to Kim.

Kim's jaw dropped. "You two are gonna do what?"

We were sitting on the couch with Kim between us.

"We're going to get married on Friday," Maeve repeated slowly.

Kim's nod of acceptance became a confused shake of her head. "But the wedding won't be until spring?"

"The wedding will be in late spring or early summer," I said.

Kim closed her eyes and pursed her lips. Maeve and I waited. Kim opened one eye and said to Maeve,

"So you two are going to get married now but hold the wedding later."

"Yes, that's what we're going to do," Maeve said with a patient smile.

Kim smiled and shrugged. "Sounds cool to me. Most people get married at their wedding, but what the heck."

"Kim, I want you there with us. Cynthia's coming down. I want you to be there too."

Maeve's relief that Kim accepted our plan was clear in her voice.

"Just try to keep me away," Kim said. "I haven't been watching out for you all this time to miss out on this."

Kim left for work. Maeve decided we should skip going to the library so we could talk to our folks. She called her mom first, holding the phone so I could hear, too.

"Let me make sure I understand what you're thinking," Phyllis said. "You're going to get married on Friday, by a Justice of the Peace, but you still plan to have a wedding in the spring."

"Yes, Mom, that's our plan. Actually, we'll be married by a magistrate," Maeve said.

"And you're going to get married now instead of waiting because you're living together like a married couple, so you feel you should be a married couple," Phyllis said.

Maeve hesitated and then tried to explain. "We aren't exactly living like a married couple, Mom. Mike stays at the apartment, but he sleeps on the couch."

She left out the part about her sleeping with me on the couch most nights." And we do have a chaperone in Kim. Otherwise, yes, Mom, that's one of the reasons."

"I see," Phyllis said. "And you think everyone will still come to the wedding next spring even though you're getting married now."

"We figure they'll come for the free food and a couple of days at the beach, if for no other reason," Maeve said.

I started to say something at that point. Before I could get the words out, Maeve kicked me. Not hard, but hard enough to let me know to keep my mouth shut.

"You may be right about that," Phyllis said. "If this is what you want to do, your father and I will support it. I know you don't need our permission or anything, but after a little thought, it doesn't sound like a bad idea. I know your father will be happier if you're married and sharing that apartment than not married and sharing that apartment. He can be a bit old-fashioned. Does Cynthia know?"

"I called her earlier to ask if she'd come down and be one of our witnesses," Maeve said.

"I would've thought Kim could do that," Phyllis said.

"Kim's going to be there. I wanted my big sister there, too."

"Should your father and I plan on coming down? Are you having any kind of dinner afterward or anything?"

"Actually, Mom, right after the ceremony, Mike

and I are leaving for River Dream. We're working at the Family Sailing Camp this weekend."

"That doesn't sound like much of a honeymoon, dear," Phyllis said.

Maeve smiled and looked at me. "Don't worry, Mom. We're planning an extravagant honeymoon next summer. Trust me."

"All right, dear," Phyllis said. "I think I can explain all this to your father."

Then it was my turn. I reached for the phone. Maeve stopped me and handed me my car keys. With a deep sigh, I took them, and we headed out to the car.

My father met us in the driveway. "Well, to what do we owe this surprise?"

"Can't we just stop by for a visit?" I asked.

My sister Malori, who'd followed him down the steps, answered first. "That would be out of the ordinary. You must want something."

"Now Malori," my mom scolded from the deck. "Do not be rude. Come in, you two. Do not let Owen keep you down there all night."

"Thank you, Eunice," Maeve said, stopping to hug Malori before climbing the stairs. "Malori, we don't want anything. We've come to tell you something."

Once we were inside and seated in the living room, we told them. They listened carefully, without comment, until we were done.

"It makes perfect sense to me," Malori said. "Who's going to pick me up, and at what time?"

I hadn't expected that. "Whoa, Malori, no one's going to pick you up."

"Oh, I think somebody better pick me up. I plan to be there when I finally, officially, get a big sister after all these years of putting up with you, big brother."

"The thing is, Mal, Maeve and I are going straight to the airport from the service. We have to be at Camp by supper."

"Then Hans or Derrick can bring me home." To Malori, it was a problem easily solved.

Maeve interjected. "We'll ask them, Malori."

"Maeve, your parents are not going to be there, correct?" Mom asked.

"That's right, Eunice. My sister is coming down, but not my folks."

My father offered a solution to Malori's transportation problem. "We could drop Malori at the courthouse and pick her up after you're done."

"That would be okay with me," I said. Having thought about it, I was glad Malori would be there.

Maeve was too. "I think that would be super. Malori, I'm glad you want to come."

"Hey, we're going to be sisters. I don't want to miss out on that," Malori said.

My father groaned. "Now I have to figure out how to explain all this to your Grandma Lillian."

Grandma Lillian was my father's mother.

"I am sure you will figure out a way, dear," Mom said.

CHAPTER SIXTEEN

November 1983

Harsh fluorescent lighting did nothing to ease the sterile setting of the Magistrate's office. The gray carpeting, speckled white walls, and suspended ceiling gave the room a neutral feel better suited to an automotive showroom than a place to get married.

But it was in just that setting, on Friday afternoon, that Maeve and I were married by a magistrate at the New Hanover County Courthouse with Hans, Derrick, Cynthia, Kim, and Malori as our witnesses.

When the Magistrate began with, "Dearly beloved, we are gathered here today..." the gray carpet and speckled white walls faded from view, and all I could see was Maeve. Reflected in her heather blue eyes were all the love, hope, and happiness overflowing in my heart. We vowed to love, honor, and cherish one another as long as we both would live. The magistrate pronounced us husband and wife, said, "Mr. Lanier, you may kiss your bride," and it was real. Maeve and I went from being Maeve and I to being us. I put my arms around her, pressed my lips to hers, and kissed my wonderful, beautiful bride.

Forever and a heartbeat later, we parted and noticed the applause. Maeve blushed. I smiled proudly.

Hans stepped up and slapped me on the back. "Man, that was some kiss. We thought you'd never come up for air."

Maeve and I went straight from the courthouse to the airport. Maeve bounded out of the GTO without waiting for me to come around and open her door. "I can't wait to get to River Dream. You have no idea."

Since I felt the same way, and I hoped, for the same reason, I said, "I think I have some idea."

"Maybe you do, and maybe you don't," Maeve said, with a suggestive wiggle of her hips. Then she noticed the look on my face. "Hmm, maybe you do."

"Our bags on the plane, babe," I said. "Let's go home."

Maeve looked at me with a puzzled expression. Then she realized I didn't mean the apartment. "Yes, Michael, take me home to River Dream."

I was tickled by the way Maeve stood on the front porch when we arrived. She greeted the house with an enthusiastic, "River Dream, I have returned," like she was McArthur at Leyte Island. Literally sweeping her off her feet, I carried her over the threshold and to the main bedroom. We'd shared the queen-sized bed before but not as husband and wife.

Later, I went out to the front porch to get our

luggage. Carrying them into the bedroom, I was wishing we had more time before we had to get to camp.

Maeve waited until I'd dropped the bags at the foot of the bed before wrapping her arms around me. "Mike, I'm so glad to be home. Does that sound funny? I mean, wouldn't most people tell me our home is that apartment in Wilmington? But not to me. River Dream is home to me."

Hugging her tight against me, I said, "This is our home, Maeve. The apartment - well, for now - it's our home away from home."

Maeve glanced at the digital clock on the nightstand and said, "I guess we'd better get over to Camp. We've probably missed supper."

My eyes widened in mock horror. "I hope not. I'm starving."

We didn't miss supper. The cook, Miss Gladys, knowing we'd show up sooner or later, kept aside a couple of burgers and some fries for us. Gladys was a great cook and always looked out for me. She'd been around Camp since before my first visit when I was a little kid.

Mr. Cooper, the camp director, insisted she'd worked as a cook in the White House during the Eisenhower administration. I never worked up the nerve to ask her. It would be akin to asking a lady her age, which my dad taught me a gentleman never does.

Family Sailing School was like Adult Sailing School, except it included children. The curriculum was similar. Because it was two weeks later in the fall, it got dark earlier. We couldn't get the campers on the water Friday evening.

Maeve and I were the last to leave the dining hall. Captain Jack was waiting for us outside the door. "Since the rest of my crew is busy helping the campers sign in, I reckon you two can take turns showing the families to their cabins."

Maeve smiled and curtsied, earning a chuckle from Jack. "We'd be glad to, Captain."

We didn't mind. It gave us a chance to get to know the new sailors while showing them around.

Camp Riversail was built as a summer camp where kids could learn to sail. Over the years its mission grew to include teaching swimming, canoeing, and kayaking. Eventually, week-long camps on marine science and conservation started being offered.

I fell in love with Camp Riversail the minute I set foot on the grounds. I told my dad when he came to pick me up I wanted to live there forever. My dad took my words to heart and, through my trust, started acquiring the land adjacent to the camp for me. He also helped my trustee set up two endowments for the camp - one to support the sailing program, and one to begin the marine science program. There have been annual contributions to both from the trust ever since.

Over the years, renovations and replacements were made necessary by wear and tear, storm damage, and growth in the camp's popularity. Since Camp Riversail was primarily a summer camp, the cabins were designed to house large numbers of adolescent children. The cabins were laid out in pods, three cabins around a bathhouse.

The pods were arranged so that each cabin faced the river. This was partly for the view, but mostly for the airflow. Gravel trails paved with quarry rock and seashell fragments crisscrossed the camp and connected the pods to all the other sites on camp.

Some of the other sites included the dining hall, the sailing center, and the swimming hole. The dining hall was a legend among Camp Riversail alumni. It's been said that the food at camp alone was worth the price of admission.

The staff cabins were nicer than the camper cabins. They needed to be, since most of the staff stayed at camp pretty much seven days a week all summer.

To accommodate families, the rooms in the camper cabins had been divided with a heavy tarp hung down the center, converting each room into two units for four. Families larger than four got a cabin to themselves.

The first family to arrive was the Bosemans, from Greenville. Carl taught at East Carolina University. Shirley was a CPA and a partner in her own firm. Their sons, Rick, fourteen, and Jay, twelve, had done some sailing at Boy Scout summer camp.

Eddie and Carol, who'd just been to Adult Sailing School, returned with their thirteen-year-old daughter, Jessica.

All told, we had seven families and a total of twenty-five student sailors registered for that weekend. Unlike the previous weekend, which had consisted almost exclusively of novice sailors, this group had a broad spectrum of abilities. Each family would have its own boat and instructor, so this would not pose a problem. To make sure everyone covered everything, though, all the participants attended all the classroom sessions.

Since we wouldn't be able to go out on the water, we'd planned an icebreaker in the Camp Life Center. Captain Jack introduced the chief instructor, Joel Chapman, a recent graduate of East Carolina University. Joel - who as a kid growing up in Mystic, Connecticut - learned to sail on Long Island Sound - introduced the rest of the staff. It felt odd not having Chase there.

After the staff were introduced, Jack invited a representative from each family to tell where they were from, a little something about their family, and why they had come to Sailing School. When the introductions were complete, Jack let each family know which instructor had been assigned to their boat.

Maeve was lucky to get Eddie and Carol. They already knew each other, and those two had some experience. Jack planned it that way since it was Maeve's first foray as an instructor.

I was assigned to the Bosemans. While the boys knew a little about sailing, their parents were complete novices. My instructing skills would get a good workout.

Maeve and I found a moment to talk to Jack about

Maeve's pay arrangements while the campers were getting to know each other. "Jack, it only makes sense for me to volunteer. Mike volunteers his time, and I am married to him. Besides, you did say you'd pay me twice what you pay him, remember? This way you can tell people you really are."

Jack's brows rose, and his eyes widened in surprise. "Married! Now when did that happen? Never mind. Time for that later. Maeve, if that's the way you want it, I can go along with that. There are other items in the budget I can use those funds for."

He cocked his head towards me. "Like for fiberglass repair every time Mike runs one of my Scotts into the dock."

"Jack, I haven't done that in almost two weeks."

"That's only because you haven't been here for two weeks." Before I could protest further, Jack patted me on the shoulder. "Mike, you know I'm just kidding."

The social broke up about nine. Maeve and I headed to River Dream. After a long, intimate soak in our Jacuzzi, we snuggled under a blanket on the front porch swing. Sipping some of Maeve's herbal tea, we listened to the night sounds on the river. The thrum from the diesel engines of a shrimp trawler headed downriver, invisible except for its navigation lights, was a slow, rhythmic backbeat to the chirping crickets.

"Mike?" Maeve asked.

"Yes, babe."

"I'm sure glad you came up and said hello in the library that night."

I tightened my arm around her. "Me too."

She pressed her head back against my shoulder. "Can you think of any place you'd rather be right now?"

Sitting there, in the place I loved best, with the woman I loved most, I couldn't think of anyplace I'd rather be. "Nope."

Maeve softly stroked my cheek, her fingertips exploring the stubble of unshaven whiskers. "You're a man of few words tonight."

I leaned into her touch, a contented smile curling my lips. "Yup."

Maeve chuckled. "Methinks thou art falling asleep, my prince. Perhaps I should take you to bed."

My drowsiness evaporated. "That is a splendid idea."

CHAPTER SEVENTEEN

November 1983

The next morning dawned cold and overcast. The air temperature was only in the high forties. It would not be a good day to capsize. It would be a good day to stay in bed, snuggled up with my new bride.

Maeve put her arms around me and shivered. "Who forgot to turn on the heat?"

Pulling our blanket up tighter, I teased her a bit. "What heat? This is a summer cottage. There's no heat."

Fixing me with a withering stare, she said, "Puhlease, tell me you are kidding."

"I'm kidding. The thermostat's on a timer. Heat should be coming on directly. In the meantime, I brewed some coffee."

Maeve eyed me suspiciously. "You made coffee?

When did you get up and make coffee?"

That hurt my feelings. "What do you mean, 'You made coffee'? You're not the only one around here who can boil water without burning it."

"I know you can brew coffee," Maeve said. "But when did you brew coffee? I never felt you get out of bed."

"I didn't," I said. "The coffee maker has a timer, too, remember. It should be started up just about now."

Maeve stuck her tongue out at me. "You think you're so smart."

"I was smart enough to marry you," I said, before leaning toward her and nipping at her tongue. The nip turned into a kiss, and the coffee had to wait. There are other ways to warm up in the morning.

Sitting at the kitchen table, gingerly sipping at the coffee I'd brewed, Maeve commented on the bare state of our cupboards. "I suppose at some point we'll need to go shopping. The coffee's the only thing that hasn't expired."

Since we got three square meals a day at Camp, I didn't see the urgency. "What more do we need? Miss Gladys feeds us."

Maeve explained the urgency. "Yes, for now. But this is the last week of Camp until spring. What are we going to do next weekend, and the weekend after that?"

Deciding being facetious would be more fun than agreeing with her, I said, "I'll order pizza."

"You know someone who'll deliver pizza out here?" Maeve asked.

I could tell she didn't think I did, and she was right. "Well, now that you mention it, no."

Maeve rolled her eyes and shook her head. "As I said, we'll have to do some grocery shopping next time we come home."

"That means a trip into the sprawling metropolis of Arapaho proper for a visit to Belangia's."

"Who-what-ee-a's?" Maeve asked.

"No, silly, Belangia's. It's the grocery store in Arapaho. You don't remember it? It's the only grocery store of any size around unless we drive to New Bern."

Maeve considered what that might mean. "I suppose we could stop at the Big Star before we come up and bring the food with us."

I was aghast at the very idea. "What, and miss a trip to the big city? You haven't lived until you've been to Arapaho, my dear."

Maeve laughed. "Alright, you nut. We'll wait and go shopping at Who-what-ee-a's."

"Belangia's," I said.

By the time we arrived at camp, breakfast was about to be served. We joined our boat crews and got in line. Tables were assigned by boat crew. Being there were so few of us, we ate in the small dining room. Captain Jack, as a concession to our matrimonial state, assigned my crew and Maeve's to sit together. Ten could sit at one of those long tables. Jack took the empty seat at ours.

Breakfast was pancakes, sausage, grits, biscuits, juice, coffee, and milk. We ate country style, passing the plate around. If you took the last helping, you had to take the plate to the kitchen for a refill. I always seemed to be unlucky when my turn came, but I smiled and never complained. Besides, it was always good to see Miss Gladys.

When I took the first empty plate into the kitchen, Miss Gladys greeted me with a hearty, "Mornin', Michael. What do you need more of this morning?"

"I need some more of those fluffy pancakes of yours, Miss Gladys."

After handing me the plate, she changed the subject. "Mr. Cooper told me you done gone and asked Maeve to marry you. I remember that summer when you two went around here like love-struck teenagers." Miss Gladys laughed at the memory. "I reckon that's because you were love-struck teenagers."

"Yes, ma'am, I sure did. Not only that, we've done gone and gotten married." I don't know why, but whenever I talked to Miss Gladys, I found myself talking like her, too.

"Then congratulations, young man. She'll sure make you a pretty wife. Don't know what kind of a husband you'll make, though. Always traipsing out here to camp to go sailing with these folks."

"I don't think she'll mind that too much, Miss Gladys. As a matter of fact, she's traipsed out here with me this weekend. Captain Jack gave her Chase's old job."

A slight frown creased Miss Gladys' face. "I was so sorry to hear that young man wouldn't be coming back no more. He's a fine fellow. I've known him as long as I've known you, Michael."

Returning quickly to her good humor, she continued. "I reckon it's a good thing Maeve's a sailor, too. She'll be able to go along when you get the urge to pull up anchor and head downriver."

Maeve came in with the empty sausage plate. "I plan to, Miss Gladys. You can count on that."

"Well, now, here she is herself. I guess I should congratulate you too, young lady. Though I don't know what you see in this rascal here. I've known him since he was in knickers, so to speak. The stories I could tell you."

"Now, Miss Gladys, don't go giving away all my secrets."

Miss Gladys gave me a warm smile. "Oh, Michael, you know I'm just telling stories on you. Maeve, Michael's a good boy who's grown into a fine young man. You couldn't do much better. Now, you two get back out there. Folks are waiting for their breakfast."

We headed back to the table with our plates of fresh pancakes and sausage.

"What happened?" Eddie asked. "Did Miss Gladys make you cook it yourself?"

"No," Maeve said as she handed the plate of sausages to Eddie. "She was filling me in on this fellow I married."

Carol relieved Eddie of the plate before he helped himself to too many.

"That's what took so long," she said. "You were telling him you've changed your mind."

"As it turns out," Maeve said, "Miss Gladys assured me I could have done worse in picking a husband. She said Mike's okay."

I stood there listening to them poke fun at me. "Well, thank you all very much. Just for that, I think I'll eat all the pancakes myself."

Jack shook his head and reached for the plate. "Don't plan on it. I'm ready for seconds."

They all laughed. I surrendered the plate of pancakes. As I sat down, I looked across the table. The way Maeve looked back at me sent a warm feeling right through me.

I gave her my best smile and mouthed, 'I love you.'

She smiled and mouthed back, 'I know. Me too, you.'

The campers stayed in the dining hall for their first class with Captain Jack. Joel took the rest of us out to get the Scotts ready for the morning sail. We carted the sails from the sail loft down to the end of the dock.

With the help of the skiff we call the Enterprise, the Scotts were moved from their mooring posts up to the dock. Normally we'd just jump in the water and walk them in, but it was too cold. By the time Jack took the budding sailors to the sail loft to pick up life jackets, the temperature had barely climbed to the mid-fifties.

"Okay, folks, find your sailing instructor. He," Jack tilted his head toward Maeve, "or she, will direct you to your boat. This morning, you'll be shown how to rig the boat for sail. This afternoon, it will be your turn. Pay careful attention and ask questions if you're not sure how they're doing something. Let's go sailing!"

I rounded up the Bosemans. Our boat was lucky

number 7. They brought the sails aboard, and I showed them how to rig the mainsail and jib. I showed them how to raise and lower the centerboard and rudder. Soon it was time to back away from the dock and get underway.

Once we cleared the dock, lowered the centerboard, and got past the other boats, I started rotating the Bosemans through each position. They all had a chance to work the helm, the mainsheet, and the jib sheets through a series of tacks.

Once they were comfortable with that, we tried a few jibes. Jibing is the more dangerous of the two turning maneuvers. We practiced it until everyone made at least one clean jibe. Then we practiced getting in and out of irons.

"Why is it called being in irons?" Jay asked.

"It's called irons because you're locked in place and can't go forward. Like being thrown in irons and locked in the brig," I said.

"So, it's not something you do on purpose?" Rick said.

As the boat floated to a stop, I turned to Rick. "Well, now, sometimes you do. For instance, if someone falls overboard, you need to turn the boat around and come to a stop right next to them so you can pick 'em up."

Rick's brow wrinkled as he considered this. Carl asked the next obvious question.

"How do we get started again, now that we stopped?"

I gestured toward the jib sheet in the cleat by his

hand. "Pull that jib sheet around the mast and the jib will backfill." Turning to Shirley at the helm, I added, "As soon as the jib fills, push the tiller hard over. Scotts are easy to get out of irons. As soon as the main catches air, trim up the jib and center the tiller. We'll sail right away."

We practiced getting out of irons until it was time for lunch. Carl was at the helm when we headed in. I let him stay until we were close to the dock before taking over and bringing us the rest of the way in. My crew had done well, and I told them so.

The light wind we enjoyed all morning gave way to livelier air by lunch. Captain Jack said we'd be doing some heavy air sailing that afternoon. He warned us to keep a weather eye out as the forecast was rather iffy.

On the way to the dining hall, I asked Maeve how her crew had done.

"Eddie and Carol took about a minute to get back into the groove. Jessica picked it up like an old pro. She really has a feel for it. I wish we could get her onto an Aqua Finn; I'll bet she could dance across the water on one."

Losing a bit of steam, she took a deep breath and asked, "How did your guys do?"

"Carl and Shirley did well. Rick and Jay impressed me. They paid close attention and asked good questions. Jay has a strong sense of the wind."

Captain Jack caught up with us. "Sounds like your folks are doing well, too. No real problems reported by anyone. This afternoon will be a proper test, especially if we get heavy air. I just hope it doesn't go and rain."

Miss Gladys prepared a lunch of tomato soup and grilled cheese sandwiches. A perfect lunch on such a chilly day. After lunch, the campers had another class with Captain Jack before going back out on the water.

That afternoon they sailed a three-corner course, practicing their tacking and jibing skills. The wind was heavier than in the morning, but that made it more fun.

The campers found the afternoon's exercises challenging, more so as the day wore on and the wind kept freshening. Captain Jack halted sailing earlier than usual when the wind gusts reached over 25 knots. Since the forecast promised worsening storms, we got ready to ferry the boats into the protected moorings of the creek. The good news was that the forecast called for the wind to swing around to the west-northwest by morning. Though that would mean chilly temperatures, it would bring sunshine and good sailing.

Jack and I were on the last boat. Maeve and Joel took the boat tied up closest to shore. Instead of sailing it out past the mooring posts, Joel tried to sail through them, like he was slalom racing.

"That boy's gonna run into one of those posts," Jack said, getting to his feet.

Joel was good, and he had just about cleared the last post when the wind died, luffing his mainsail. That caused his mainsheet to go slack and swing right toward the mooring post.

CHAPTER EIGHTEEN

November 1983

"Joel, tighten up the main," Maeve called out, but it was too late. The mainsheet tangled around the mooring post, and before either Joel or Maeve could get to their feet, the Scott's momentum pulled it over on its side, dumping them both in the water. They disappeared beneath the surface just as the mainsail slapped down over the spot where they'd gone in.

Jack turned our boat into the wind, bringing us to a stop several yards outside the last mooring post.

"Do you see 'em, Mike?" Jack's voice was calm, but I could hear the worry he was trying hard not to show.

Before I could answer, a sputtering head of soaked strawberry-blond hair broke the surface.

"Maeve," I hollered, "are you okay?"

"I'm okay!" she called back. "What about Joel?"

"I don't see him," I answered.

Jack and I both started calling his name. Instead of swimming toward our boat or shore, Maeve stripped off her life jacket and jack-knifed below the surface.

Jack slapped the gunwale and said, "Dammit, what's she think she's doing?"

"She's looking for Joel," I said. I stripped off my life vest, stopping only to pull my Ka-bar folding knife from the zippered pocket, and rolled off the rail into the water.

When I surfaced, I could hear Maeve yelling at Captain Jack. "Joel is tangled in the jib sheet. I can't get it outta the cleat."

"Michael's on his way," Jack assured her.

With a few powerful strokes, I reached Maeve's side. "Show me."

Maeve grabbed my hand and pulled me under the water. Visibility was never good in the Neuse, and we found Joel more by feel than sight. I swam close enough to see his face.

Joel wasn't panicking yet, but his eyes bulged in a way that told me he was close. He pointed down. I let some of the precious air out of my lungs and sank down to where I could see and feel the jib sheet wrapped around his leg. Knowing Maeve had tried the cleat, I didn't waste time trying to loosen it. Taking hold of the line just below Joel's knee, I made quick work of it with my knife.

As soon as he felt the line slip from his leg, Joel gave a couple of powerful kicks and shot to the surface, only to have his head run smack into the mainsail. I came up next to him, and we pushed the sail up enough to catch our breath.

"Thanks, Mike," Joel said before being racked with a coughing fit.

From beyond the edge of the sail I heard Maeve ask, "Are you two all right?"

I looked at Joel and cocked my head, eyebrows arched in question. He stifled his coughing long enough to nod.

"We're okay," I called.

"You're okay," Jack hollered. "But how's my Scott?"

Joel and I looked at each other and laughed.

"It's gonna need a new jib sheet," I shouted. Turning to Joel, I said, "You sure you're okay?"

"Other than a little rope burn and swallowing a little too much of the Neuse." After another cough, he took a deep breath, dove, and swam out from under the sail.

Maeve and Joel swam to shore, where the nurse was waiting to look at Joel. I clambered back aboard the boat with Jack, and we sailed onto the creek. Jack took a crew out on the chase boat to recover the capsized Scott. I went to check on Maeve and Joel.

Maeve was walking with Joel to the staff cabin when I caught up with them.

Putting my arm around Joel, I asked, "So, what did the nurse say? You gonna mutate into some kind of Aquaman after swallowing all that river water?"

Joel shook his head and laughed. "Nothing like that. Other than an upset stomach, I should be fine."

Maeve gave me a shove. "Quit picking on him. He

had a close call."

Joel gave her a weak smile. "It's okay, Maeve. He deserves to give me grief. He's the one who cut me loose."

"So, what are you gonna do now that we're done sailing for the day?" I asked Joel.

"I think I'll grab a shower and then take a nap." A wry grin crossed his lips. "I don't know why, but I'm worn out."

Joel's mention of a shower reminded me that Maeve and I had both been in the river. After seeing Joel back to the staff cabin, Maeve asked me, "So, what do we do with ourselves now?"

When an overabundance of wind cut sailing short, Captain Jack would hold the classes ordinarily given on day two. That way, the time could be spent on the water, weather permitting, the second day. The best part of the plan was that it only involved Jack and Joel. The rest of the staff got the afternoon off.

"I was thinking we could go home, have a hot bath and then ..." I said with a sly grin.

"And then ...?" Maeve asked expectantly.

"And then go to Belangia's," I answered while helping her into the Jeep.

Maeve looked perplexed, and perhaps a bit disappointed. "That's your plan?"

Raising my eyebrows, I replied, "Well, that's part of my plan."

Maeve smiled. "That's better. I thought I was losing my touch for a minute."

A few minutes later, we were at the house. Heavy

raindrops splattered the windshield. Since I hadn't put the doors on the Jeep - they were still in the shed - this posed a problem.

"I need to take the Jeep to the shed to put the doors on. It won't take long. I'll check the tie-downs while I'm there. This storm is only gonna get worse."

"I'll come with you," Maeve said.

I saw no reason both of us should get soaked. "I have a better idea. Why don't you go in, make a pot of tea, fire up the woodstove, and be waiting for me when I get back?"

"No, wait, I have a better idea," Maeve said with an innocent grin. "Why don't I go on in, make a pot of tea, fire up the woodstove, and be waiting for you when you get back?" Maeve said, grinning.

"Now who's a brat? Go on in. I'll be right back."

Heavy raindrops began pelting Maeve as she got to the screened porch. Reaching down, my fingers brushed my key clip, and I realized she didn't have a key to the door. She realized it at the same moment and turned to glare at me. I jumped out of the Jeep and ran the key to her through the deluge, getting drenched. She laughed.

"I'm glad you think it's funny. While we're in town, we need to get you a key made."

"Yes," she said, stifling her laughter. "That would be a good idea."

After wiping my eyes with the back of my hand, I unlocked the door and let her in. Then I ran through the rain a second time, got in the all-too-open Jeep, and headed for the shed.

Before installing the doors on the Jeep, I checked on *Sky Dream*. The Cessna was rocking a bit in the wind, but the tie-downs were secure. I got the doors on the Jeep - too late to keep it from getting soaked inside - and headed back to the house.

Torrential rain drenched me again as I ran to the porch. A jagged bolt of lightning lit up the dreary afternoon sky as I reached for the doorknob, followed by a rumble of thunder that rattled the windows. Turning to look out at the river, I could see whitecaps churning the water.

Maeve left a bath towel on the porch swing for me. Clearly, she meant for me to dry off before going in. I stripped off my wet clothes, dried myself as best I could, and wrapped the towel around my waist before going inside.

I found her waiting in the kitchen with two mugs of steaming Earl Gray tea.

"My goodness, you're sopping wet," Maeve said.

As I reached for my tea, I said, "I left my wet clothes on the porch."

She pulled the mug out of my reach. "You need to finish drying off first. Come with me to the bedroom and I'll get you another towel."

We went into the bedroom. Maeve got a dry towel from the bathroom, and eventually, it was used to finish drying me.

We rested under the comforter for a while, listening to the rain on the roof before Maeve picked her robe up off the floor and went to the kitchen to warm up our tea. I put on some sweats.

Maeve had moved to the living room and was curled up on the couch. There was a small fire going in the woodstove.

Maeve held her arms out and said, "Come sit with me. The fire will keep you warm outside, and the tea will warm you inside."

We snuggled close. The warmth of the fire chased away the chill.

Handing me my mug of tea, she asked, "Now isn't this better, nice and warm and cozy?"

"Um hm," I murmured in reply.

I turned to lie with my back against the arm of the couch. Maeve curled up against me with her head on my chest.

"Mike, you know what?"

"What?" I asked, softly stroking her hair.

Maeve gestured towards the ceiling. "You can watch the rain through the skylight. It's really kind of neat."

Looking up, I noticed she was right.

"Do you know what else?" Maeve asked as she pulled my arm tighter around her.

I smiled and gave her a gentle squeeze. "What else?"

"I'm very happy on this couch with you right now."

A warm feeling came over me that had nothing to do with the fire or the tea.

"Are you? I'm glad. I'm very happy to be here with you right now."

For a while, we didn't say anything. The only sounds were the crackling of the wood burning in the stove and the rain pattering on the roof. We finished our tea, the warmth spreading through us. I would have fallen asleep if Maeve hadn't stirred. I opened my eyes to see her looking up at me.

"Michael, if we're going to town, we'd better get going."

Not wanting to end the close moment we were enjoying, but realizing she was right, I sighed and stretched. "I think the rain has let up some."

"It sounds like it. What time does What-who-ee-ahs close?" she asked.

"I don't know. Seven or eight, I guess. Why?"

Looking at the clock on the VCR, she said, "Because it's almost six. If we don't hurry, we may have to drive all the way to New Bern to find an open grocery store."

"Why don't we just go out to eat?" I asked.

The look Maeve gave me squelched that idea quickly. "We can't just go out to eat because I want to cook you a home-cooked meal. Even back in town, I've never cooked for you. It's about time I did. So, let's go to What-who-ee-ahs so I can buy what I need to make dinner. Besides, we need more coffee."

"Well, why didn't you say so in the first place?"

Upon learning we were out of coffee, I leaped from the couch and quickly changed into some jeans. Maeve had to get herself presentable before we could leave. Not that she used much make-up - she didn't need it - but she wanted to tame her hair some.

As we headed out the door, I ran back into the bathroom and grabbed an old bath towel.

"What's that for?" Maeve asked.

"I'll use it to dry off the Jeep seats. I'm sure they're still wet," I said, gesturing to the still falling rain.

I didn't have an umbrella, so we made a dash for the Jeep. The rain had let up some, but there was still a light drizzle. I opened Maeve's door and ran the towel over her seat before going around and repeating the process on my side.

"It's a good thing these aren't cloth seats, or they'd take forever to dry," I said.

Climbing in, we headed out for Belangia's. By the time we got there, the rain had all but stopped.

Belangia's was not a big grocery store, but it had the essentials. Maeve could find everything she needed.

She decided to cook steak with mashed potatoes and green beans. For dessert, she bought one of their fresh-baked apple pies and some vanilla ice cream. She added some essentials to the cart, like paper goods, coffee, tea, a small carton of milk, and other staples that would last a while in the cupboard. Finally, she declared we had everything we needed. We checked out and headed home.

Once home, Maeve went about setting up housekeeping in the kitchen. It was a pleasure watching her figure out what was going to go where.

"Don't just sit there watching me. Help me get some of this stuff put away. The sooner I get this kitchen organized, the sooner you get dinner."

The storm made our first taste of domestic life possible. I reveled in it as I helped her get dinner ready.

We ate at the kitchen table. As yet, there was no

dining room table in the dining room. We didn't care. This was the first meal we cooked in our own home and ate at our own table. After dinner, we washed the dishes in our sink, put them away in our cupboard, and went into our living room to watch our television.

"I'm surprised you have cable all the way out here," Maeve said.

My face scrunched into a grimace as I recalled the bill. "I'd hate to tell you what it cost to get the cable company to run the line for just this one house."

I don't remember what we watched, just that Maeve fell asleep with her head on my shoulder. I woke her gently.

"Sweetie, I think it's time to go to bed."

We were soon snuggled up together under our own comforter in our own bed, falling asleep. Over us, the winds changed, and the skies cleared.

The next day dawned crisp, clear, and cold. It was barely forty degrees when the alarm went off. I slipped into my robe and went to the kitchen for a cup of coffee while Maeve got dressed. It had just started brewing, so I left my empty mug on the counter and went back to the bedroom to get myself properly dressed for the day.

Maeve was pulling on a green sweatshirt with a gold Seahawk and the letters UNCW on the front. "Make sure you put on an extra layer, Mike. It's going to be cold out there on the water."

"Yes, dear. I'll be sure to do that."

She pretended to ignore my sarcastic tone. "Did you start the coffee?"

"I set it last night, dear."

Maeve grabbed a pillow off the bed and tossed it at me.

"Brat. Hurry and get dressed. We don't want to miss breakfast."

She was right. We didn't want to miss breakfast.

Dressed for a chilly day on the water, we poured our coffee and headed over to camp. The cold air seemed to energize everyone. The conversation was buzzing over breakfast. Several folks had gone to eat at the Trawl Door restaurant in Oriental. They were comparing notes on the dishes they'd tried.

Right after breakfast, since they'd completed their class work during the previous afternoon's rainstorm, we got on the water. Because of the cold, we did not practice the capsize drill. Instead, we reviewed what to do in the event a boat capsized.

We did practice bringing a boat alongside a mooring and crew overboard drills. After lunch we worked sailing away from and back to the dock. There was some bumping, but no major collisions, with the dock or between the boats. All too soon, it was time to de-rig the boats, say goodbye to our new sailors, and sail the Scotts up the creek for winter.

After the Red Books were signed, check-out was done, and the campers had all gone home, the staff gathered in the dining hall for a debriefing and farewell.

Captain Jack stood, hands on hips, and slowly scanned the staff, his face a stern mask. "Once again, you did a fair job of making novice sailors out of non-sailors. I reckon we can call this weekend a moderate success." He could only keep a straight face so long.

"You did a great job. I couldn't have asked for a better crew. I'm gonna miss you bunch of rascals. You all better be coming back in the spring."

Mr. Cooper stopped in to tell us how much he appreciated all we'd done. He invited us to return anytime. Contact info and hugs were exchanged. We all promised to stay in touch.

Maeve and I went back to River Dream and put things in order for our absence over the coming week. We packed up what we needed to take back to Wilmington, boarded *Sky Dream*, and headed on our way.

On the flight back to Wilmington, I gave Maeve a chance to practice her flying skills.

"We really need to get you into a proper class so you can get your license."

"A month ago, I would have said that was crazy talk," Maeve said. "Now I can't wait."

I talked her through most of the approach to ILM but took over for the actual landing. After making sure *Sky Dream* would be serviced and ready for our next flight, we climbed into the GTO and headed for the apartment.

CHAPTER NINETEEN

November 1983

My sleep was broken by the incessant jangling of the telephone at six the next morning. Phone calls at that hour of the morning are almost never good things.

I reached across Maeve and picked up the phone. Barely had I said "Hello" than Derrick's agitated voice came spilling from the handset. "Mike, thank God you're there! Man, I need to talk. I need some help."

A dread chill swept over my skin at Derrick's panicked tone. Adrenalin surged into my system, and suddenly I was wide awake. "Derrick, what is it? What happened?"

"Mike, man, it's my dad. He's in the hospital."

I struggled to keep my voice calm. "What happened, Derrick?"

"I don't know much. Just that he got hurt on his way home from work. Mike, I've gotta get home, man."

"I'm on it, Derrick. Sit tight. I'll be right there."

Maeve, now awake too, rolled over and asked, "What's going on? Is something wrong with Derrick?"

I climbed out of the double bed we'd squeezed into Maeve's room when we decided to get married. I filled her in as I hurried to get dressed.

"It's Derrick's dad. He's in the hospital."

"What happened?"

"He didn't have any details. All Derrick knew was his dad got hurt on his way home from work."

Maeve sat up abruptly. "Isn't Derrick's dad a cop?"

"He is, but I don't know if that has anything to do with what happened."

I finished dressing and kissed Maeve. "I'll call you as soon as I know something more."

When I got to the dorm, Derrick was pacing back and forth across the room. "Mike, man, what am I going to do? My mom just called again and said Dad is unconscious from a head wound. She said he stumbled on a robbery on the way home and got jumped. Punk hit him with a board. He hit him with a board, man! Mike, I gotta get home."

"I'll get you home, Derrick. First, I need to make some calls. Then we have to get someone to take a note to your professors letting them know what's happened. Maybe Jerome next door will do it." I was trying to sound calm and organized, thinking it might help Derrick calm down.

He stopped pacing and sat down at his desk. "Okay,

Mike, I know you know what to do. What are you gonna do?"

Relieved he'd stopped pacing, I outlined my plan. "I'm going to call the airport and ask them to get my plane ready. Then, I'm going to write a note for Jerome to give to our professors. Then, I'm gonna call Maeve, let her know what's going on, and ask her to pack me an overnight bag. While I do all that, you're going to pack an overnight bag."

As I got done what I needed to get done, Derrick put a few things together in a gym bag. Maeve packed me a bag, and we picked it up on the way to the airport. She made me promise to call her with updates. When we arrived at the airport, I made one more call, this one to my dad.

"Dad, Derrick's dad's in the hospital. I'm flying him to Nags Head. Is there any way you can have a car waiting for us there?"

"Of course, Michael. Of course I will. Tell Derrick we'll say a prayer for his dad."

"Thanks, Dad, I'll tell him. I love you, Dad." Under the circumstances, it seemed important to let my father know that.

As we walked into the hangar towards my twin engine Piper Seneca, Derrick stopped, pointed at the Seneca, and looked at me. "Mike, are you about to fly me to Nags Head in that plane?"

"Well, yeah. It's a lot faster than the Cessna," I said.

Shaking his head, Derrick followed me on board. I did a preflight check, started the engines, contacted the tower, and soon we were taking off.

Clear skies and light winds aloft made for an easy flight up the coast. After we landed at the Manteo airport, I called Maeve. She'd already left for class, but the answering machine picked up.

"Hi, babe. Derrick and I got here okay. As soon as I look into getting the plane refueled, I'm gonna find out if my dad was able to get us wheels. I'll call as soon as I know more. I love you."

When I checked, there was no car waiting. The gentleman at the general aviation counter told me there was a taxi outside waiting to pick up a Mr. Lanier and Mr. Carson. The taxi took us to the hospital where Derrick's dad was.

Derrick's mother looked up, startled, when we burst into the waiting room. "Derrick, how did you get here so fast?"

After hugging his mother, Derrick explained. "Mike flew me up here in his plane, Mom. How's Dad, Mom?"

"The doctors say he just came around just before you came in. He was asking what was going on and why he was in the hospital." Relief was evident in her voice.

Derrick visibly relaxed. "Oh, thank God. I was so afraid."

"We were all afraid, honey. But it sounds like he's going to be all right," Mrs. Carson said.

Derrick looked down the hall. "When will we be able to see him?"

Mrs. Carson nodded toward the nurses' station. "I asked the doctor that. He told me it would be a little while longer, but not to worry, I'd be able to see him soon."

While Derrick was talking to his mom, I noticed several other folks in the waiting room. Some were wearing police uniforms. Others were in civilian clothes but were clearly armed.

A tall, distinguished gentleman in plain clothes approached me. "Are you Derrick's friend Mike? Did I hear him say you flew him here?"

"Yes, sir, I'm Mike, and yes, sir, I flew him up here in my family's plane." I couldn't tell if he was pleased or upset that I'd brought Derrick.

Holding out his hand, he said, "We are much obliged to you, son. For a while there we thought we might lose Derrick's daddy."

I took his hand just as Mrs. Carson said, "Heavens, Leon, tell Michael who you are."

"My apologies, Mike. I'm Derrick's uncle, Leon Carson. His daddy is my baby brother."

"Uncle Leon, you know Daddy hates it when you call him baby brother," Derrick said as he walked over and stood beside me.

Leon's face broke into a grin. "That's too bad. He is my baby brother. He should be used to it by now. He's been my baby brother his whole life."

Hoping to learn more about what happened, I asked, "Mr. Carson, how did Derrick's father wind up in the hospital?"

Derrick's uncle gave me an appraising stare before relating what he knew.

"As near as we've been able to determine, John

walked into that store to buy a soda on his way home from work, like he does every day. Only this time, three punks were robbing the place when he walked in."

John Carson, Derrick's father, was a sergeant on the Nag's Head Police Department.

As Derrick and I sat, giving him our rapt attention, his Uncle Leon told us what he knew of the incident that landed Derrick's dad in the hospital. As near as the police had figured out from the surveillance tapes, Sergeant Carson walked into the Quik-Pick, like he did most every night when he was on second shift. This time, there was a man standing at the counter with a piece of pipe in his hand. Another man appeared to be rifling the register. The clerk was nowhere in sight.

Seeing he'd interrupted a robbery in progress, Sergeant Carson drew his service revolver and ordered the men at the counter to put their weapons down and their hands up. Then he keyed his walkie-talkie to alert dispatch to what was going on and that he needed backup.

As the perpetrator at the counter turned toward him and laid his pipe on the counter, a third crook came into camera range and struck Sergeant Carson from behind with a piece of lumber. Sergeant Carson fell to his knees and was struck a second time.

The robbers at the counter must've decided it was time to cut and run. They grabbed one more handful of change out of the register and ran out past Sergeant Carson's prone body. The crook with the pipe hit him once more for good measure. The three men then escaped in a construction company truck.

Backup arrived on the scene a short time later. Finding Sergeant Carson unconscious, they called for an ambulance. The dispatcher, a friend of Mrs. Carson, called and told her John was hurt and on his way to the hospital. Mrs. Carson called Derrick before leaving for the hospital. When she arrived, Leon was already there.

"The perpetrators are already in custody," Leon said. "They left us plenty of clues. Almost made it too easy."

The store's video surveillance cameras caught the whole crime. By the time Derrick and I arrived, the police had already reviewed the tape and identified the suspects. As Leon said, it was almost too easy. The robbers were all wearing their work jackets, emblazoned with their employer's name over one pocket and their own first names over the other. The truck they escaped in was also a company truck. It took detectives less than an hour after viewing the tape to get arrest warrants and place all three in custody.

When he'd finished relating the story, the look on Leon's face told us exactly what he thought of the perpetrators. "If they'd surrendered, they might have gotten off easy. Now they're up for assault of an officer with intent to kill. The DA will make it stick, too, with the video showing the second perp hitting Johnny when he was down."

While Uncle Leon was filling us in, the doctor came out and told Mrs. Carson she could see her husband. A little while later she came out and told us he wanted to see Derrick and me.

Derrick's father was sitting up in the hospital bed when we walked in. He was still hooked up to the monitors, but the oxygen tubes had been removed.

"I get a little bump on the head, everybody panics, and you two decide to use it as an excuse to play hooky and skip school."

I could tell by the stunned look on his face the last thing Derrick expected was a scolding. "But Dad, Mom called, really worried. You were in the hospital unconscious."

Derrick didn't notice it at first, but I saw the smile breaking across his father's face, even though he tried to hide it.

"I know, son, and I'm real glad you're here. Come give your old man a hug."

Derrick smiled, shook his head, and went over and hugged his dad.

"What did the doctors say, Dad? You're going to be all right, right?"

"Yeah, I'll be all right," his dad said. "I have a pretty hard head. Where it really hurts is where the son-of-a-gun first hit me across the shoulders. At least he didn't break anything. Your momma tells me they have the guys who did it. That was fast work."

"They do, Dad. Uncle Leon says they left behind a trail of clues like breadcrumbs. How long are the doctors going to keep you in the hospital?"

Sergeant Carson shrugged, which made him wince. "They say they want to keep me overnight for observation. I suppose I'll have to put up with it."

"Then I guess I'll stick around until you get out tomorrow," Derrick said.

"Oh no you don't, son," his dad informed him, shaking his head slowly. "Your mother said Michael flew you up here."

Sergeant Carson paused and turned to me. "Thank you very much for that, by the way, Michael. Not too many folks would have done that."

He turned his attention back to Derrick. "Now you can fly right back and not miss any more school."

"But, Dad," Derrick tried to argue.

Sergeant Carson would have none of it. "No buts, son. You boys need to get back to school. Now go on. Tell me goodbye, then go send your Uncle Leon in. I'll be fine. Your mother will keep you up to date on my condition, I'm sure. Go on now, git."

Derrick hugged his dad again, told him he loved him, and walked out. When I started to follow him, Sergeant Carson told me to wait.

"Michael, I meant what I said. You must be a good friend to Derrick. Not many people would drop everything, get in their private plane, and fly a friend a couple hundred miles. I want to thank you for that."

I felt myself choking up and fought to control it. "I'm just glad I could, sir. Derrick's been a good friend to me. I have a lot of acquaintances but few people I consider genuine friends. I count Derrick on that very short list."

Sergeant Carson nodded. "Well, as far as I'm concerned, you're one of the family now. Now git, before I get all mushy about it. Get on back to school."

"Yes, sir," I said, resisting the urge to salute.

I passed Leon on my way back to the lobby. He stopped to thank me again for bringing Derrick home. Derrick was talking to his mother when I walked into the lobby.

"Your daddy's right, Derrick. You and Michael need to get back to school. Your daddy's gonna be all right. There's no need for you to miss any more classes on his account."

Derrick must've realized she wasn't going to change her mind. "Okay, Mom, we'll go back."

"That's better," Mrs. Carson said, apparently satisfied that Derrick was going to be reasonable.

Turning to me, she said, "Now, Michael, you better come back with Derrick another time, under happier circumstances. And bring that pretty little wife of yours too; we'd like to meet her. Oh, yes, Derrick told us about her."

Derrick's eyes widened, and he shrugged helplessly. "What can I say, man? A boy can't keep secrets from his mom."

Smiling, Mrs. Carson hugged Derrick. "That's right, and don't you forget it. Michael, thank you again for bringing Derrick all the way out here. I know it seems like we're trying to rush you right on back to school, and we are, but we sure are glad you came."

After assuring us again that everything would be all right, and she'd call if there were any unexpected changes, we said our goodbyes and left the hospital. Our taxi was gone. There was a squad car waiting for us with a tall, attractive female officer standing next to it.

"I've been ordered to take you two gentlemen into custody and see to it that you return directly to the airport, board your plane, and get off our island," the officer said. "In your case, Derrick, I use the term gentleman advisedly."

I was a little taken aback. Derrick started laughing. I waited for him to tell me what was going on.

"Mike, this cantankerous old policewoman is my cousin, Paula. Don't let her scare you. She almost never shoots people she's just met. How are you, cousin?"

Paula stepped up to hug Derrick.

"I'm doing much better now that I know your dad is gonna be okay. How are you doing, Derrick?"

Derrick sighed and looked back at the hospital. "It's like you said, now that I know Dad's going to be okay, I'm doing fine. Are you really here to take us to the airport?"

"To take you and make sure you get off safely," Paula said, gesturing towards the police cruiser.

"Is there any chance you can take us somewhere for lunch first?" Derrick asked.

Paula thought about that for a moment. "If you promise to behave, I suppose so. Where do you wanna go?"

"Well, since we are here on the Outer Banks, with all these wonderful seafood places, how about the Rib Shack? Does that sound good to you, Mike?"

"Sounds good to me," I said, rolling my eyes.

Paula shook her head. "I shoulda known."

While we ate lunch, I learned that Derrick's Uncle Leon was Paula's father. Paula had twelve years on the force, having joined after a four-year hitch as an Army MP. I told her I was a fellow veteran. Paula said she wouldn't hold being in the Navy against me.

She'd been married once. The guy didn't like being married to a cop, so he left her for a cocktail waitress up in Norfolk. She hadn't been in any serious relationships since then. It'd been eight years, and she didn't see that changing.

After lunch, Paula drove us to the airport, and we flew back to Wilmington. Before boarding, I called the apartment and left a message letting Maeve know Derrick's father was going to be all right and we were headed back to town.

Once we'd achieved level flight, Derrick turned to me and said, "Mike, don't you just love Mondays?"

"No, Derrick, as a matter of fact, I don't like Mondays much at all."

CHAPTER TWENTY

November 1983

By the time I got to the apartment, Maeve had already left for class. She left me a note to meet her at the Nest for supper before I went to the library.

I was worn out and wanted nothing more than to take a nap. Instead, I grabbed my books and headed for the Nest. If nothing else, it would be good to stretch my legs after spending all that time in the plane.

Maeve was waiting for me at the Nest. "I was wondering if you'd make it. I wasn't sure what time you'd get back."

Setting my books down on the table, I said, "I got to the apartment just in time to read your note, grab my books, and hoof it on over here."

"You made it just in time. I was about to start without you," Maeve said. "I'm glad Derrick's father's going to be all right. So, what happened?"

I filled her in on the details as Derrick's Uncle

Leon had related them to me and added what more I'd learned from Paula.

"So, what's this Paula like?" Maeve asked, trying to sound nonchalant.

"Jealous?" I asked.

"Curious," Maeve said.

"The first thing you notice about Paula is she's tall. She must be close to six foot four. She wears her hair cut short. I hardly had a chance to talk to her. Derrick spent most of the time trying to get details his Uncle Leon may have left out."

Maeve motioned for me to continue as she took a bite of her grilled chicken.

"One person I didn't see, who I thought would be there, was Derrick's sister. She's a high school senior. Mrs. Carson told me they made her go to school. I can't imagine she got any work done. But Sergeant and Mrs. Carson are pretty serious about school."

"How do you mean?" Maeve asked.

"When Derrick and I went in to see his dad, once Sergeant Carson convinced Derrick that he was okay, he told Derrick to get back to school. Then when we came out, Mrs. Carson emphasized how important it was that we get back here so we wouldn't miss any more school."

"Well, what's wrong with that?" Maeve asked. "I think it's a good thing."

Looking at my plate, I tried to decide if I wanted to finish my fries. Lifting my gaze to meet Maeve's eyes, I replied, "I suppose so. It just seemed a little odd under the circumstances. I asked Derrick about it. He said they'd always been that way."

We finished supper and headed to the library. On the way, Maeve passed along a message I'd received while at Nag's Head.

"One of your *people* called today."

It took a second to understand what she meant.

"One of my people called. You mean from the trustee's office?"

"That's where he said he was calling from. Your *person* said to tell you that the documents were ready for closing and to call to schedule a time. What are you getting ready to close?"

I realized the cat was out of the bag. "Rats! I wish he hadn't said anything about that. It was supposed to be a surprise."

Maeve's brow furrowed, and her lips curled into a frown. "Exactly what kind of surprise, Michael?"

"Uh, I sort of bought you a little something," I said.

"Oh, you bought me a little what?" Maeve asked, her voice bordering between irritation and amusement.

"I bought you a little house," I said, trying to make it sound like it was no big deal.

Maeve stopped in her tracks, grabbed my arm, and spun me around to face her. "You did what?"

"Well, it's like this, sweetheart. You know the Nadeaus are trying to sell their house because of John's new job in Charleston. And the apartment's too small for Kim and both of us. With the housing market like it is right now, John and Jenny would probably have trouble finding a buyer.

"I know you'll like their house. It's sound side, on the water. I thought it would be a win-win situation for all of us. John and Jenny could quit worrying about selling the place. You and I will have a nice place to stay when we're in town. In the long run, it's a great investment. Sooner or later, the market is going to improve."

For a moment, Maeve just looked at me, shaking her head. "You really are something. Most guys would buy their wives jewelry or perfume. Mine buys me a house. You really are something, Michael."

Maeve's tone and the sparkle in her blue eyes let me know she was pleased. The kiss she gave me, right there on the sidewalk in the middle of campus, told me she was more than just pleased.

"I'm glad you approve, but now I have a new problem."

Cocking her head to one side, Maeve asked, "Oh, what is that?"

"Well, I was going to surprise you with the house for Christmas. Now I have to find something else."

"You brat," Maeve said. But she smiled as she took my hand, and we finished our walk to the library.

Later, as I fell into an exhausted sleep, I thought to myself, Considering how this day started off, it didn't end too badly. All's well that ends well.

CHAPTER TWENTY-ONE

November 1983

The closing on the Nadeau house occurred on the Thursday afternoon before my birthday. I'd worked out a deal with John and Jenny so they could stay in the house until the start of Christmas break. They could've left earlier, but Jenny wanted to finish out the semester.

Maeve and I did not attend the closing. A person from the trust took care of it. I thought it would have been awkward for me to be there.

Shortly after that, Veteran's Day rolled around - my birthday. November 11 was on a Sunday, with the holiday observed on Monday. That meant no school for Maeve and me. We flew up to spend the long weekend at River Dream.

Maeve had a surprise waiting for me at home. I

didn't get my first hint that anything was up until we flew over River Dream and I noticed what appeared to be several tents set up on the lawn.

"What're those things doing there?" I asked, a trifle annoyed.

Maeve craned her neck to look out the window of the Cessna. "Oh, what, the dining flies? Good, they got them up." She sounded like she expected them to be there.

Smelling a rat, I inquired further. "Just what do you mean, 'Good they got them up'? You were expecting them to be here?" I tried to keep a level tone.

Giving me a stern look, Maeve said, "Now, don't get upset. I invited a few people to come up for your birthday. Your folks, my folks, some friends."

"I see. Who else is in on this?"

Looking a little sheepish, Maeve said, "Well, your mom and dad helped me with the planning and execution. I mean, we're a long way from anywhere out here. I had to make arrangements for folks."

"Arrangements, what type of arrangements?" Realizing I'd been had, I began feeling amused at Maeve's vague explanation.

"Look, Mike, this was supposed to be a surprise. I didn't think about the dining flies already being up when we got here."

I laughed in spite of myself. "Well, it worked. I'm surprised all to pieces."

"Then, can we quit circling and land?" Maeve asked. "There's still lots I've got to do to get ready."

As I lined up to land, I noticed several cars making

their way down Camp Road. The first in line looked like Derrick's '72 Malibu. His car was kind of hard to miss - orange with a black vinyl roof. It turned off for Camp Riversail just as I got the plane back to the shelter.

Seeing him at camp explained why Derrick had begged off on lunch earlier. Realizing the arrangements Maeve made involved Camp Riversail, I thought to myself that I should have overflown the camp to see who else's car might be parked there.

While helping Maeve down from the plane, I said, "Well, I guess we're even in the surprise department. You found out early about the Nadeau house, and I learned early about this shindig you have planned. And here I was hoping for a nice, peaceful, long weekend away from it all."

"Now, Mike, don't you go all curmudgeon on me. You are going to have a great time. All of your friends and family came all this way to celebrate with you. So you will have a good time, you understand?"

"Yes, ma'am. I'll have a good time, ma'am. I promise," I said in my most mischievous tone.

"Oh, I'll ma'am you all right, right in the shin," Maeve said. But she smiled when she said it.

Once we tied the plane down, Maeve got into the driver's seat of the Jeep.

"I'll drop you at the house, and then I've got to see a man about a pig," she said.

That's just what she did. It was the first time I remember her driving the Jeep. I took our bags into the house, unpacked, and wondered what to do with myself.

Deciding I didn't want to sit around, I left Maeve a note and headed down to the dock. *Geddaway*, my 26-foot Hunter sailboat, was up on the lift. My old Mariner, *Riverscape*, the boat Maeve had first sailed with me, was afloat and tied up on the lee side of the dock.

The tarp over the cockpit was easy enough to remove. I didn't intend to sail. The sails were still in the storage chest on the dock. Besides, I wasn't dressed for the conditions. It felt good just to be aboard.

I felt bad my own boats had been sitting there all fall without being sailed. After all the sailing I'd done over the summer, they must have felt I'd abandoned them. That would have to change in the spring.

It was all well and good to spend time jaunting about the river just off Camp Riversail teaching sailing, but I needed to take a couple of days and go sailing. Not that I wanted to go anywhere in particular; I just wanted to be out on the water.

Opening the hatch, I ducked down into the cabin. It wasn't big. I couldn't quite stand up straight. But it was enough if you just wanted to get out of the sun or go for an overnight sail. For longer trips, there was *Geddaway*.

I checked over everything, and all seemed in order. After making a mental note to myself to pull her out of the water before we left, I closed the cockpit, replaced the tarp, and headed back up the dock.

To my surprise, my dad was coming down the dock toward me. "I figured I'd find you down here when Maeve told me she'd left you alone."

I nodded over my shoulder back toward the boats. "I was thinking I'd put *Geddaway* in the water and sail to the Outer Banks for the weekend."

He smiled a crooked smile and raised his brow. "You'd have several very upset women on your hands if you did. Maeve and your mother have been planning this for weeks. Even before you two eloped."

"Is that so? And how long have you known about it?" I asked.

"Oh, I've been in on it from the beginning," he said. "Maeve needed me to square things with Mr. Cooper over at Camp, among other things."

"You could've given me a heads up," I said, trying to sound irritated.

My father looked at me like I was crazy. "Not without taking my life into my hands." He held up the keys to my fishing boat, a 20-foot Grady-White Dolphin. "Maeve said maybe you and I should do a little fishing."

Puzzled by the suggestion, I said, "It's nearly dark."

"Don't tell me you can't navigate between here and Dawson Creek in the dark?"

He knew very well that I could. It was practically a straight line.

"Of course I can, but what's at Dawson Creek?"

I looked over my father's shoulder and saw Derrick coming across the road.

"All right, men," Derrick said. "Are we going fishing or what?"

Realizing it would be futile to resist, I gave in.

"If you guys want to motor around on the river in the dark, then let's go." I reached down and loosened the boat cover on the Dolphin.

We boarded, fired up the engine, and motored away from the dock. I was worried the engine wouldn't start, considering how long it'd been since I'd last run it. My worries were for nothing. It started up after coughing and clearing its throat.

Since it was dark, I made sure the running lights were on and eased slowly out to the channel. On the water, the wind seemed colder. I wished I'd brought a heavier coat.

"Man, it's chilly out here. I wish I'd brought a heavier jacket," Derrick said.

"I was just thinking the same thing," I told him.

My dad called from his seat near the bow, "You guys are soft. I find it invigorating."

Invigorated or not, he shivered when he said it.

We motored sedately down the river toward Dawson Creek. There weren't many lights along the river. Most of the land between Camp and Dawson Creek was part of the Neuse River Conservation Area, a non-profit I set up with a good part of the land around River Dream. The only part of River Dream that wasn't in the conservancy was the land around the airstrip, the house, and the dock.

"Well, there's the Dawson Creek Bridge. Should we go on to Oriental and have dinner at the Trawl Door?" I asked.

My father laughed, then shook his head. "I would strongly recommend against that. I think your mother and your missus have something special planned for tonight's meal."

"And what would that be?" I had a pretty good idea what it might be.

My mother made great lasagna. She didn't make it often, but my birthday was one of those rare occasions when she did. If that was what was in the plan, then we needed to get back to River Dream pronto.

"I think you can guess. What does your mother always make for your birthday?" my dad asked.

"In that case, let's get on back."

I may have run the boat back at a higher speed than was prudent, but my dad didn't complain, and Derrick seemed to enjoy it. Soon, we were tied up at the dock and headed for the house.

It looked like all the lights in the house were on. Besides my father's Suburban and Derrick's car, I noticed the Jeep, and a Subaru sedan I didn't recognize, in the driveway.

"Whose green car is that?" I asked.

Looking to see which car I meant, Derrick said, "I think that's Maeve's sister's car." He wrinkled his nose. "She's kind of unfriendly."

"She's not bad, just reserved. Besides," I said, giving him a friendly pat on the back, "she's too old for you."

Derrick laughed and gave me a playful shove. "I wasn't thinking of dating her."

"You weren't thinking of dating who?" Maeve asked.

We hadn't noticed her standing on the porch. Evidently, she'd heard at least part of our conversation.

"Cynthia," I said. "Derrick doesn't think your sister likes him much."

"Don't worry, Derrick. She just doesn't know you like we do," Maeve said. "Now, why don't y'all come and have a seat in the dining room?"

I was wondering how we were all going to sit in the dining room. The last time I checked before I headed down to the dock, we didn't have any dining room furniture.

Well, now we did. I don't know where it came from or how it got there, but there it was - a beautiful white oak dining room table and 6 chairs. It fit well in the room and matched the décor to a T. I just stood and stared.

"Excuse me, but who put that dining room table in my dining room?" I asked.

Maeve took my hand and with a bright smile explained.

"Don't you remember, honey? You asked me to help you finish furnishing the house. I saw this at Rose Brothers and thought it would be perfect."

"How did it get here? I mean, how did it get here since I dropped off our stuff?" I realized I needed to be specific with my question.

My mother took up the story. "It was on the back porch. You just did not see it. Derrick and your father moved it in while you were moping in your sailboat. Then the girls and I moved in the chairs, set the table, and arranged the rest of this stuff while the guys took you out joyriding."

"For the record, I was not moping. I was checking to make sure everything was ship-shape before I pull her out for the winter."

My mom folded her arms across her chest and smiled. "Whatever you say, dear."

"Well, do you like it?" Maeve asked, spreading her arms to encompass the room.

There was only one right answer to that. "It's perfect. I guess this means we'll definitely be using this as a dining room."

"In that case, isn't it about time we dined?" my father asked. "I'm famished."

Food was brought out, drinks were poured, we took our seats, and the blessing was said. Before we could enjoy the lasagna, my mother insisted we eat a garden salad.

When my mom made lasagna, I always ate more than I should. I would've eaten more, but we'd finished it.

Pushing back from the table, I looked around and noticed someone was absent. "By the way, not that I miss her or anything, but where is Malori?"

Still in her seat, my mother put her hands on her hips. "It is about time you noticed that your precious baby sister is not here."

"I didn't know I had a new baby sister. I was talking about Malori."

My mom tried hard to keep a straight face. "Maeve, you see what a brat he can be."

"I've gotten used to it, Eunice," Maeve said, with a slightly exaggerated sigh.

My dad filled me in. "Mike, your sister's spending the night at your grandmother's house. She'll come with your Aunt Donna and cousin Denise tomorrow."

Aunt Donna lived next door to Grandma Lillian in Rhems, just south of New Bern.

"Yes, your sister decided she would rather spend the evening hanging out with her cousin than putting up with a bunch of old folks," my mother said. "Congratulations, Michael and Maeve, you are now officially old folks."

"My mom and dad, and Derrick's mom and dad, will be here tomorrow, too," Maeve said as she rose to clear the table.

Getting to my feet to help her, I asked, "Just what is going to go on tomorrow?"

My dad cleared his throat, stood, and bowed to my mother. "In honor of the 23rd anniversary of the laborious day your mother gave birth to you, we are going to celebrate her efforts on your behalf with a pig picking."

At this, Cynthia, who'd just taken a sip of her drink, nearly choked with laughter. It startled us all. She'd hardly said a word during dinner.

"Oh, excuse me. That was the most interesting way to describe someone's birthday I've ever heard."

"Please, Cynthia, do not encourage him." My mother turned to Maeve. "At least you can see where Michael gets it."

Maeve chuckled. "Yes, I think so. But if they weren't who they are, would we love them as much?"

My mom's lips twisted, and she stared at the ceiling for a moment. "Hmm, undoubtedly not. I guess we will just have to put up with them."

My father and I exchanged looks of utter innocence and then broke down laughing. Derrick and Cynthia looked at each other and grinned. Maeve and Mom looked triumphant. I looked down the table at Maeve and blew her a kiss.

CHAPTER TWENTY-TWO

Many hands made quick work of cleaning up after dinner.

"Where did all this stuff come from?" I asked, taking in all the new gadgets on the counters.

"The toaster oven and microwave are gifts from your mom," Maeve said. "Cynthia brought the blender. The new coffee maker is courtesy of your father."

Maeve and I were the last to leave the kitchen. We found my folks in the living room. My dad was adding wood to the fire in the woodstove. Derrick and Cynthia were nowhere to be seen.

"Those two went for a walk on the dock. It's such a calm, clear night, Derrick told Cynthia she could count the stars by their reflection in the river," my father told us before we could ask.

"Derrick said that, did he? When did he become such a poet?" I was astonished at the idea.

"Perhaps Cynthia inspired it in him. They hit it off pretty well over dinner," Maeve said.

"How could you tell?" I asked. "Neither of them said more than two words."

"I know my sister," Maeve said.

I gestured towards the front door. "Well, should we put on our coats and join them? I've heard tell you can count the stars on the river on a calm, clear night like this."

"Derrick must be a good poet; people are already stealing his lines," Maeve said.

We laughed, got our coats out of the hall closet, and stepped out into the night. It was clear, calm, and cold. The temperature had dropped ten degrees since we returned from our diversionary cruise.

As we stepped off the porch, I noticed Derrick and Cynthia standing shoulder to shoulder at the end of the dock. Derrick appeared to be pointing something out and, as I followed his hand, I noticed the sound of aircraft. He was pointing out a formation coming from the direction of Cherry Point Marine Corps Air Station. They must have been practicing night flying.

I nudged Maeve and pointed out how cozy Derrick and Cynthia looked, but she'd already noticed. Maeve had one of those crooked smiles on her face, a little 'I told you so' and a little 'well will you look at that.' I took in a breath to holler out to them, but Maeve, sensing what I was about to do, put a cautioning hand on my shoulder. Instead, we walked quietly down the dock to join them.

I never tired of the river at night. "It's a beautiful view, isn't it?"

"Yes, so peaceful, serene," Cynthia answered, without turning around.

"When there's no wind, like tonight, you can see the stars reflected on the river," Derrick said.

"I've heard," I said, earning myself a stern look from Maeve.

"Mike and I love it here. If it weren't for school, I don't think we'd ever leave."

Cynthia's chest rose as she took a deep breath of night air. "I can understand that. I envy you, Maeve. All this, and someone to share it with."

I noticed Derrick looking at Cynthia, who was looking out at the river. Maeve looked at me, at Derrick, at Cynthia, and then back at me.

I mouthed, "What?"

Maeve shrugged, as if to say she didn't know what to think either. Then she shivered a bit as a gust of wind rippled the water.

"I think we should head inside," I said.

Cynthia crossed her arms over her chest and moved closer to Derrick. He put his arm around her shoulders.

"It is getting colder," Derrick said. "When the wind picks up, it bites right through you. You're right, Mike. We should go in."

"I think so too," said Cynthia. "I'm not really dressed for this."

Cynthia and Derrick turned and walked back to

the house, his arm still around her shoulder. They didn't move apart until they stopped so he could open the door for her.

Maeve turned to me, one eyebrow raised. "What do you know about that?"

By the time Maeve and I reached the house, my mom and dad were ready to call it a night. I expected them to head off to Camp to stay in one of the cabins. Was I in for a surprise. They headed instead through the den towards the front bedroom, grinning like the cats that caught the canaries. Curiosity overwhelmed me, so I followed them.

It turned out the dining room wasn't the only room Maeve found time to furnish. In place of the old double bed and chest of drawers, a beautiful cherry bedroom set now filled the front bedroom, along with matching bedspread and curtains in a seashell motif. Maeve walked in and stood beside me.

"What do you think?" she asked.

"I think somebody's had too much time on her hands," I said. "I think I need to talk to your professors about giving you more homework."

"Maeve, that means he loves it," my mother assured her.

Taking Maeve into my arms, I said, "Yes, sweetheart, I love it. But how did you sneak it in here without me knowing about it?"

"Maeve didn't actually sneak it in. That was my job," my father said. "I met the furniture truck here yesterday. Your mom and I spent the night in New Bern. We had them leave the dining room set on the back porch but went ahead and put this in here. Maeve said you never go into this room."

My mother spoke up and admitted, "I brought the curtains and bedding with us, so that it would be all made up before you got here."

Looking around at them all, I said, "I'm the victim of a huge conspiracy. Is it a good thing my parents and my wife can cook up schemes like this to surprise me?"

"You'd better get used to it," Maeve said. Then she threw her arms around me and gave me a big kiss. "Happy birthday, babe, I love you."

My dad chuckled and shook his head. "Why don't you two get out of here so your mother and I can get ready for bed?"

Maeve and I bid them goodnight and went back to the living room. Much to our surprise, we found Derrick and Cynthia sitting together on the couch, his arm once again around her shoulders. They were watching an old movie on the television.

I cleared my throat as we walked in. "May we join you?"

Derrick jumped as if I'd shocked him and snatched his arm from around Cynthia's shoulder. After a sheepish look at Maeve, he moved to an easy chair near the hall door.

Cynthia mustered a little more dignity. She gave Derrick a sideways glare and moved to the Boston Rocker by the window.

Maeve and I studiously avoided looking at each other, afraid we'd start laughing; however, we couldn't hide our smiles as we took their spot on the couch.

"What are we watching?" Maeve asked.

"That old Bogart and Bacall movie, *Key Largo*," Cynthia said.

I winked at Maeve and said, "That's a classic love story. Perfect for setting a romantic mood."

Cynthia turned red. Derrick tried to disappear into his chair. Maeve nearly choked trying not to laugh out loud.

"Actually, I think it's about time I headed over to Camp for the night," Derrick said. "Cindy, do you need a ride?"

"Yes, Derrick, thank you. It is getting late," Cynthia said.

"Awe, c'mon guys, don't rush off. We'll make some tea, throw another log on, and finish the movie," I said, hoping to make amends.

"Please stay a little while, y'all." Maeve gave me a stern look. "We'll behave, I promise."

Derrick deferred to Cynthia. "What do you think, Cindy? Maybe it's not that late."

"We'll stay as long as they behave," Cynthia said, glaring fiercely at Maeve and me. "Then can I catch that ride?"

"It will be my pleasure," Derrick said with a bow.

I almost said something then but, through a Herculean effort, kept my mouth shut. The way Maeve looked at me, it was a good thing I did, too.

They stayed. Maeve made some tea. I popped some popcorn. We watched the rest of the movie, and then Derrick gave Cynthia a ride back to Camp. I checked the wood stove and banked the coals. It was going to be a frosty morning. I wanted to get a fire going early. Then, Maeve and I got ready for bed.

"Who is this imaginary girl Cindy that Derrick was talking to?" I asked.

"What? Oh yeah, that surprised me, too. She's never let anyone get away with calling her Cindy."

"I gave Derrick a heads up about that, too," I said.

"It's a mystery, all right," Maeve said. "What do you make of it?"

"I think it means she likes him."

Maeve's furrowed brow and pursed lips told me she thought I was way off base. "Well, Derrick is a likable guy, but...you mean, LIKES him."

I shrugged and tried again. "Maybe. Or she's just being nice about it. Figures it's not worth making an issue about if she's never going to see him again."

Maeve shook her head. "I don't think that's it. I think maybe she does like him. But I don't think she LIKES him. She's a lot older than he is."

"Either she does, or she doesn't," I said. "That's Derrick's problem. It's who the other Dalton girl loves that I'm worried about."

Maeve held her arms out to me. "Maybe you'd better come over here and remind me why I love you."

She didn't have to tell me twice.

CHAPTER TWENTY-THREE

November 1983

The next morning, I woke with a start. Someone was making noise in the kitchen, but I could feel Maeve beside me. Slowly, I remembered my mom and dad spent the night in the newly re-furnished front bedroom. One of them was probably prowling the kitchen. Most likely my dad. He was an early riser.

Getting out of bed quietly, I made my way to the kitchen. Sure enough, my dad was pouring himself a cup of freshly brewed coffee.

He raised his mug when he saw me coming into the kitchen. "Good morning, Mike. Coffee's ready."

Taking my blue and gold GO NAVY mug from the rack over the sink, I said, "Looks like you found everything all right."

"I had to look through a few cabinets, but finally

found the coffee and filters right over the coffeemaker. That's a funny place for them to be."

"Don't blame me. I just live here," I said. "I had nothing to do with arranging the cupboards."

I poured myself a cup of coffee with a dollop of maple syrup for sweetener.

"You're not upset about the new furniture, are you?" my father asked.

Taking a seat across from him at the kitchen table, I took a cautious sip of my coffee.

"No, actually, I'm kind of glad about that, for a couple of reasons."

"Really?" He took another sip of his coffee. "And what would those be?"

Setting my cup down, I listed them for him. "First, those rooms really needed to be done. I mean, I have this great place but couldn't invite anyone up because I didn't have a decent bed for them to sleep on. And if they did come, there was no place to sit down and eat."

"That's true enough. Not that your mother and I mind staying at the Marina. But it was nice being able to sleep under your roof last night. What's the other reason?"

My lips curled into a smile. "Maeve. I'm glad she felt confident enough about us to do this. It shows me she really feels this is her home, too. Do you know what I mean?"

"Yes, I think so. I would've thought she'd be a little nervous about doing it. But when she first talked to your mother and me about arranging all this, the only thing she was nervous about was keeping it a surprise.

Son, Maeve had no doubts."

"What worries me, Dad, is how'd she pay for it?"

His eyes sparkled with amusement. "Well, she didn't. Not exactly. At least not all of it. When you began building this place, you had me set aside money for construction, furniture, maintenance, that kind of thing, remember? You can be a little anal about things like that, son. I suppose that's a good thing. You got it from your mother.

"Anyway, I explained to Maeve that the money for the furniture had already been set aside. All she needed to do was pick out what she liked. Bad news, son. Once she got used to the idea, she didn't seem to have any trouble spending your money."

I chuckled. "That's not really a problem. I need somebody to help me spend it."

"You don't have any trouble doing it yourself once you find something you really want to spend it on," my dad said. "At least I can take some pride in most of the things you've spent it on."

"Thanks, Dad. I owe any good sense I've shown to you and Mom."

He lowered his cup and looked me square in the eye. "You're okay with all this?"

"I'm okay with what I've seen so far," I said. "What else am I in for?"

My dad got up to refill his coffee cup.

"There's no more furniture as far as I know. Just an old-fashioned pig picking with your family and friends."

"I think I can handle that," I said.

After topping off my mug, I walked down to the dock to savor the morning sunshine on the river. The skies were clear, and the temperature hovered just below 40. I could feel it warming up as the sun climbed in the sky.

When I returned to the house, Maeve was sitting on the porch swing, waiting for me with her own fresh cup of coffee. My heart beat a little faster when I caught sight of her.

"Good morning, beautiful. Isn't it a gorgeous morning?"

Maeve smiled, and her eyes sparkled in the morning light. "Hmm, yes, it is. Cold though. You were up early."

I joined her on the swing and collected a good morning kiss.

"I heard a burglar prowling around our kitchen looking for coffee. It turned out to be my dad. I guess I'm not used to people staying in the house with us."

She yawned and then took a sip of her coffee. "Well, I never heard a thing. I slept like a baby."

Thoughts of my talk with my dad came to mind. "Maeve, you did a great job picking out the furniture. Thank you." I kissed her again.

"You're quite welcome. I'm glad you like it. Your mom was a big help picking it out. I'd only planned on the dining room set. Then your dad told me you'd had money put aside for furniture and that I should use it," Maeve said. "You'd mentioned a few times that I should pick out furniture for the place, so I did."

"And you did wonderfully. Now all we need to do is

figure out how to furnish the den and we'll be done," I said.

"Oh, sure, more work for me. No good deed goes unpunished," Maeve said with a smile. I decided that warranted another kiss.

I already had a pretty good idea of how I wanted to set up the den. "I won't make you do the den alone. I have some ideas. I'm thinking of desks for each of us, a big table, maybe a filing cabinet."

I could tell by the thoughtful look on her face that my plan appealed to her. "It sounds like you want to make a regular office out of it. That might be a good idea."

Smiling, I said, "Wow, that makes three."

Turning to me with a puzzled expression, she asked, "Three what?"

"Or maybe four," I said.

"Four what?" Maeve asked.

"Four good ideas I've had." I put my arm around her.

Maeve squinted and bit her lip. "I know I shouldn't ask, but here goes. What were the other three?"

"The other three what?" I asked, as if I had no clue what she was talking about.

She slapped me lightly on the shoulder. "Brat! What were the other three good ideas you had?"

"Oh, those," I said. "The first was asking you to sail *Riverscape* home with me. The second was offering to walk you home from the library that night. The third was asking you to marry me."

Maeve didn't say anything for a minute. Her blue

eyes glistened. Finally, she put her arms around me.

"Sometimes you say the most wonderful things, Michael Justin Lanier."

And then she leaned toward me and pressed her lips to mine, her mouth hungrily moving over mine, her tongue caressing my lips until they parted. Our tongues dueled and danced. I tilted my head so that I could kiss her more deeply. Her hand pressed the back of my neck, drawing me ever closer, even as I entwined my fingers in her hair to hold her to me more dearly. Breathless, we parted. Looking into Maeve's sparkling eyes, I thought, make that five good ideas.

We rose unsteadily and went inside. Not until the warmth from the woodstove hit me did I realize how cold we'd gotten sitting on the swing, smooching on the porch. The next sensation to penetrate my awareness was the smell of sausage cooking. Walking through the newly furnished dining room to the kitchen, I found my mother and father tag teaming a breakfast of pancakes and sausage. Seeing them, it hit me how hungry I was.

"Are Derrick and Cynthia coming for breakfast?" I asked.

"No," my father said. "They called while you two were necking on the porch. They're going to get breakfast at the Minnesott Grill."

Upon hearing that, Maeve's eyebrows rose. "Oh, they did, did they?"

My mom paused in her pancake flipping long enough to say, "Michael, Mr. Smith - you know him, son, Miss Gladys' husband - is outside setting up the pig cooker. Go ask him if he wants some breakfast."

My dad saved me the trip. "I already asked him, dear. Miss Gladys got up and made him a big breakfast before he left to come here this morning."

"Is Miss Gladys coming to the pig picking?" I asked.

"No," Maeve said. "She and her sister are going to New Bern today to do some shopping."

My father laughed as he placed another cooked sausage on the serving platter. "Mr. Smith said she's going there to spend all his money."

"That's what wives are supposed to do, dear," my mother informed him. "You remember that Maeve."

"Yes, ma'am, I'll keep it in mind," Maeve said, flashing me a flirty grin.

We sat down for pancakes and sausage, with real maple syrup straight from New Hampshire. Real maple syrup was hard to find in eastern North Carolina. We ordered it from my mother's cousin in Chesterfield. They shipped all over the world.

Over breakfast, my mother decided it was time to bring up something that had been on her mind for a while. "Kids, I don't mean to pry, but have you given any thought to a date?"

"Gee, Mom, we've been on lots of dates."

My father shot me a warning glance.

"That is clever, Michael. Is he not clever, Maeve?" my mom asked. Her expression and tone said she did not think it clever at all.

"Sometimes not so much. Like right now," Maeve said, agreeing with my mother's meaning rather than her words.

"Agreed. Now, as to the question of a date, have you given it any thought?"

Maeve decided it'd be better if she spoke for us. "Actually, Mom, we have."

Okay, that was new. When did Maeve start calling my mom Mom?

"And?" my mother asked.

I interrupted. "What brought this on all of a sudden?"

My father explained. "Your Grandma Lillian is coming today. I told you that last night. She's under the impression that you're going to announce your wedding date at the party. Where she got the idea, no one knows. We don't mean to push, but if you have a date in mind, today might be a good time to share it."

Grandma Lillian was a formidable woman. "That's a good reason," I said.

"Yes, it is," Maeve agreed. "Considering this is the first time I'm meeting Grandma Lillian, and I want to make a good impression."

My mother got us back to the matter at hand. "That point having been made, may I dare inquire again, have you two thought about a date?"

"We were thinking about the first Saturday of summer next summer," Maeve said. "We'll both be done with classes. I'll be done with my student teaching. We'd have all summer for our honeymoon."

"I see you have given it some thought. Quite a bit, I would say."

"We were gonna tell everyone at Thanksgiving,

once we firmed up some of the plans," I said. "Maeve, we could announce the date today, couldn't we?"

"Sure. We may not know all the details, but the date shouldn't change."

One potential complication entered my mind. "Uh, everyone who's going to be here understands that Maeve and I are already married but still plan to hold a wedding, right?"

My mother sighed and nodded slowly. "Yes, Michael, all the folks coming to your party know you and Maeve decided not to wait until your wedding to get married."

Pushing back from the table, my father said, "Okay, that sounds good to me. Dear, does that sound good to you?"

My mom sat up straight. She pushed her plate forward, placed her hands on the table, and said to my father, "As I recall, dear, I was fine waiting for the kids to let us know in their own good time."

My father cleared his throat but said nothing more. I smiled awkwardly at Maeve, and she smiled back. My father looked uncomfortable, but my mother looked smug. She scored one that morning.

Before the silence at the table became awkward, an obnoxious pre-teen voice sounded from the front door. "Hey, is anyone home around here? Little sister is on the porch."

"Malori, don't be rude," we heard Grandma Lillian say.

"I'm sorry, Grandma," Malori apologized.

Grandma Lillian, despite her gray hair and petite

stature, was the only person who could, with a glare from her piercing blue eyes and a mere word, humble Malori.

Born near Ogden, a small town outside Wilmington, Lillian lived there all her life until Grandpa Bill died. Then she moved next door to my Aunt Donna in Rhems, an unincorporated township south of New Bern. She said she did it to help Donna with my cousin, Denise. My father told me that after Grandpa Bill died, Grandma Lillian just couldn't stay in Ogden among the memories of their years together.

CHAPTER TWENTY-FOUR

Guests continued to arrive throughout the morning. Fortunately, it turned out to be one of those pleasant November days when the high just reaches seventy and the clouds stay away - a perfect day for a pig picking.

Mr. Smith had arrived early and set up his pig cooker behind the house. Cooking a whole pig - Mr. Smith told me the one he was roasting for my birthday weighed in at eighty pounds - over charcoal takes a long time. When it was time to turn the pig onto its back, a small crowd gathered around the cooker, waiting to see if Mr. Smith would pronounce the ribs ready to be picked. That's how pig pickings got their name. As the pig cooked, and each layer got done, the guests picked off the meat that was ready to eat.

I was glad Mr. Smith was cooking the pig. During the summer, he cooked a pig every Saturday at Camp. It was always delicious.

Once everyone had their fill of all the fine victuals prepared for the party, my dad gently indicated it was time for Maeve and me to announce that we'd set a date for our wedding.

Standing on the top step of the back porch, I called out to our guests. "If I could have everyone's attention. There's something Maeve and I want to share with you. As y'all know, Maeve and I got married but haven't had the wedding yet."

There were some chuckles and shaking heads.

"We're happy to announce today that we've set the date. We hope all y'all will come and share the moment with us."

Malori, having moved to the front, blurted out, "Okay, so when is it?"

I rolled my eyes and sighed. "We're getting there, sis."

Grandma Lillian shushed Malori.

Stepping up next to me, Maeve smiled and slowly turned her head to make eye contact with everyone.

"We've decided to celebrate our vows on June 23' the first Saturday of summer, next year."

Gentle applause rippled through the crowd at the announcement.

"That's wonderful," Grandma Lillian said.

"Do I get to be a bridesmaid?" Malori asked.

My eyes widened in mock surprise. "Who says

you're going to be invited?"

"Michael!" Maeve scolded me. "Of course I want you to be a bridesmaid, Malori."

The others took turns coming by to congratulate us. Since it was the first time many of them had met Maeve, they also congratulated me on finding such a wonderful lady. Certain old friends offered her their sympathies for getting stuck with me.

Derrick's mom and dad congratulated us warmly. When I asked Derrick's dad how he was doing, he told me there were no lingering effects, and he was back on full duty.

Maeve's folks came up and let us know they were pleased we'd set the date. I think they'd begun wondering if we ever would.

Grandma Lillian waited until everyone else had taken their turn before talking to us. She'd never been one to mince words.

"Well, Maeve, I'm glad I finally got to meet you, since my grandson hasn't seen fit to bring you by to meet me."

"I'm so glad to meet you, too, Mrs. Lanier. I've been looking forward to it. Please don't blame Mike that we haven't been up to see you. We've both been quite busy."

Grandma Lillian smiled and patted Maeve gently on the shoulder. "Don't go making excuses for Michael, dear. I know he stays busy. Going to school full-time, working at the camp, plus staying on top of the other pies he has so many fingers in. It's a wonder he had time to win your heart."

"Grandma, you make it sound like I'm a workaholic. I'm anything but."

"No, maybe not. But Michael, you do manage to keep busy," Grandma said. "Too busy to visit a tired old lady."

Shaking my head and arching my brow, I said, "Grandma, I don't know any tired old ladies."

"How very kind of you, Michael. Maybe there's some hope for you yet. Maeve, you must be a good influence on him."

"I hope so, Mrs. Lanier," Maeve said.

Linking arms with Maeve, Grandma said, "Please call me Grandma. Everyone does."

"Okay, Grandma," Maeve said, a delighted smile lighting her face.

"I'm glad you two picked a date. I know these are modern times, but I still believe that if a couple's going to be married, the bride should get to enjoy all the trappings of a wedding. Of course, the most important thing is that you two love each other. I can see you do, and that you do your best to make each other happy."

Blinking back the sudden moisture in my eyes, I said past the lump in my throat, "Thank you, Grandma."

The glisten in Maeve's eyes told me Grandma Lillian's words meant as much to her as she echoed me. "Yes, thank you so much."

"And Michael, before I forget, Happy Birthday," Grandma said.

My mother's timing was impeccable. No sooner

had we finished our conversation with Grandma Lillian than she announced it was time for the cakes.

Cakes - plural, I thought.

Cakes. There were several. We had several guests and needed enough to go around. There was lots of ice cream, too.

The cake decorated with birthday wishes was placed before me. It was fudge-marble with chocolate frosting, my favorite. Twenty-five candles burned on it - twenty-three candles for twenty-three years plus one for good luck and one to grow. I thought I didn't need one to grow but knew better than to say anything.

Everyone sang happy birthday. I blew out the candles, getting them all in one breath. The cakes were cut and served with the ice cream.

As had become traditional on my birthday, there were no gifts except Malori's. Malori gave me a bag of Goldfish crackers. On her birthday, I always give her a bag of Munchos chips.

The seemingly silly tradition dated back to my fourteenth birthday. Mom had asked Malori what she wanted to give me for my birthday. Malori picked out a bag of Goldfish crackers because she knew I liked them. It wasn't quite what Mom had in mind, but she went ahead with them anyway.

Much to Mom's surprise and Malori's joy, I loved the present, both because I really do like Goldfish crackers, and because I knew Malori had picked them out herself. In return, on Malori's next birthday I gave her Munchos because I knew how much she liked them. At four, Malori thought it was a perfect present. A tradition was born.

When we explained the tradition to Maeve, she kissed my cheek and said, "Michael, that's the sweetest thing I think I've ever heard of."

"Awe, c'mon, Sis, it's just a joke Mike and I play on each other," Malori said.

But she winked at me when she said it, as if to say, 'Not really, Mike, it's our special thing, okay.'

That's when a lump formed in my throat at the realization of how fully my family embraced Maeve.

This morning, Maeve called my mom, "Mom." My grandma told Maeve to call her Grandma. Now my sister was calling her Sis.

"Michael, what's wrong?" Maeve asked, her eyes narrowed in concern.

I swallowed hard and said, "Excuse me, will you?"

I escaped into the house, into the bathroom, and pulled myself together. Shortly, someone knocked at the door.

"Mike, honey, are you okay?" Maeve asked through the closed door.

I opened the door a crack and saw that she was alone.

I shrugged. "A little too much wine, I guess."

"Michael Justin Lanier, you've not touched a drop of wine since I've known you," Maeve said. Then, more gently, she asked, "What's really the matter?"

I smiled at her and pulled her close. "Nothing's the matter. I was just overwhelmed when I realized that not only do I love you, but my whole family loves you.

It's like you were meant to be a part of my life. I mean, I knew that. I believed it ever since the first time I saw you again. But today, it became so much clearer. Am I making any sense?"

In the back of my mind, I was wondering if my dream of a future with Rhiannon had been just a boyhood fantasy, and Maeve had always been my destiny.

Maeve melted into my arms and said, "Oh, Michael, you do say the most wonderful, beautiful things."

As I pressed my lips to hers, we forgot all those people in the yard. But before we could lose ourselves completely, there was another knock on the door.

"Is everything okay, you two?" my mother asked through the door.

"Yes, Mom," Maeve said with a big sigh. "Everything is better than ever. We'll be right out."

"Alright, dear," my mom said. "Some of your guests have to get going. They have long rides home. You two need to come say goodbye."

"We'll be right there, Mom," I said.

Maeve and I checked each other to make sure we were presentable and went back outside. No one said anything about our sudden disappearance.

In twos and threes, our guests left until only my folks, Maeve's folks, Derrick, and Cynthia remained. Mr. Smith had already packaged up the leftover pig for us, packed up his cooker and departed. To my surprise, most everything else had been picked up, too.

We sat down around one of the tables on the lawn.

My father came and took a seat across from me.

"I called the rental company to let them know we were done with the dining flies," he said. "They probably won't be able to get anyone out until tomorrow afternoon, but they won't charge for the extra day."

Maeve's mother, Phyllis, set a stack of cups and a pitcher of iced tea on the table.

"There are plenty of leftovers," she said. "We won't have to worry about what to have for dinner if anyone gets hungry later."

It was late afternoon, and as the sun sank toward the horizon, the air started getting chilly. When I suggested we move inside, everyone agreed.

We trekked into the house. Maeve put on the kettle for tea, and my dad made a pot of coffee. We pulled a couple of kitchen chairs into the dining room and gathered around the table.

"I think that went rather well. Do you agree, Phyllis?" my mother asked.

"It went very well, Eunice," Phyllis agreed. "Mr. Smith knows how to cook a pig."

I shouldn't have been surprised my mother and Maeve's were on a first-name basis, but I was. Maeve's parents were still Mr. and Mrs. Dalton to me. Her father's name was Theodore, but he went by Ted.

"Everyone did seem to enjoy themselves," Ted observed.

Cynthia chimed in. "I know I had a good time."

"Me too," Derrick said.

"What did you think, Mike? You were the guest of

honor. Did you have a good time?" my father asked.

Looking around, I tried to think of something to say to let them know how much the day meant to me.

"I can't thank you all enough for everything. Never have so many done so much for just me."

They rewarded my attempt at humor with polite chuckles.

"All kidding aside, I'm very touched and humbled that you went to such trouble to celebrate my birthday."

My father cleared his throat and shook his head. "Your birthday. We went to all this trouble to trick the two of you into picking a date for your wedding."

They all laughed. Even Maeve broke into a grin. Derrick laughed louder than anyone else.

I turned a wounded gaze on my former roommate. "Et tu, Derrick?"

"Sorry, dude," Derrick said. "But your dad got you good that time."

"He did, honey, admit it," Maeve said.

I said nothing and eventually, with a few last chuckles, they got themselves under control.

"Now that we know when," Phyllis said, "do you have any idea where? Your place here would be nice, but it's kind of out of the way. Don't get me wrong, it's lovely here, but it is a long way from anywhere. I'm thinking of your guests."

I understood my mother-in-law's point.

"Mrs. Dalton, you're right about River Dream being a long way from anything. That's part of its charm. You practically have to go somewhere else first to get here. However, that would be a problem for the wedding guests. After all, it'll be summer, and the cabins at Camp won't be available then."

Mrs. Dalton stopped me. "Michael, don't you think it's about time you started calling me Phyllis? After all, we are family."

"And I'm Ted, Mike," Ted added.

"Thank you both," I said. "That means a lot to me."

My father brought the discussion back to the question of where to have the wedding. "I think we agree River Dream, as nice as it is, is too remote for the wedding. The question then is, where do we have the wedding?"

"How about the Wright Isle Resort?" Cynthia asked.

Maeve nodded in approval. "Now there's a thought."

"It certainly has plenty of rooms and fine accommodations," my mother said.

Ted asked, "Isn't that the big hotel right on Wrightsville Beach?"

"That would be a lovely place," Phyllis remarked.

"Yes, Ted," my father said. "It's literally right on the beach. They have a large meeting room we could use for the ceremony, and a huge banquet hall."

Derrick spoke up. "I know a band you could book for the reception. The lead guitarist is in one of my classes. They play weddings all the time."

Almost to myself, I said, "I wonder if the place is available that weekend."

My dad gave me a puzzled look. Then he realized

what I was hinting at. Neither the Daltons, nor Derrick, nor even Maeve, knew that through the trust I owned a sizeable piece of the Wright Isle Resort. It was an issue that was about to come up.

"It sounds very nice, but wouldn't it be rather expensive?" Ted asked.

"That wouldn't really be an issue, Ted," my father said. He explained the situation. While it didn't mean we could use the place for free, expenses would only include food, drink, and wages for the help involved. Guests would get a preferential rate, and members of the wedding party would be guests of the house.

"It sounds like the perfect place to me," Phyllis said. My mom agreed.

Cynthia looked back and forth between the two moms. "You two agree. Dad and Owen seem to think it's a good idea. Derrick has no objections. I'm all for it, considering I'm the one who suggested it. There's really only one question everyone seems to be forgetting to ask."

They sat there thinking about that for a minute. Maeve and I wisely kept our mouths shut, though we knew what Cynthia was getting at.

Shrugging his shoulders, Derrick finally asked, "I give up, Cindy, what are we forgetting?"

Before Cynthia could answer, we were all drawn to the look of astonishment on Phyllis' face. She stared at Derrick for a moment, looked at Cynthia, and then back at Derrick. Ted looked a little surprised himself, but Phyllis ...

"What? Did I say something wrong?" Derrick

asked.

Phyllis shook off her surprise. "No. No, I'm sorry. No, dear, you didn't say anything wrong. It's just, I've … she's … he called you Cindy," Phyllis said, her mouth forming a confused smile. "You don't let anyone call you Cindy."

"Mom, he's been calling me Cindy all day. Hadn't you noticed? I don't mind it, really."

Phyllis' brow scrunched, and she put her hand to her chin.

"No, dear, I guess I hadn't noticed. Did you notice, Ted?"

"No, dear, I didn't. But what's the big deal? She likes him to call her Cindy, so?"

Hoping to move the discussion along, I said to Cynthia, "To get back to the question at hand, Cindy, what question is everyone forgetting to ask?"

"I don't mind Derrick calling me Cindy. To you, bro-in-law, it's Cynthia."

She was smiling like it was a joke. The hard look in her eyes, though, showed she meant it.

"Well, we seem to have reached a consensus that Mike and Maeve should have their wedding at the Wright Isle, right?"

"That's Michael to you, sis-in-law," I said under my breath.

Maeve gave me a warning kick under the table. "Shush, Michael."

Cynthia continued. "That's all well and good, but what do Michael and Maeve think of the idea?"

"You mean they get a vote?" my dad asked.

My mother rolled her eyes at him. "Of course they get a vote, Owen. After all, if they are not there, then there is no reason for the party."

"I suppose not," Dad said.

"Cynthia's right," Phyllis said. "We should ask the bride and groom what they think."

"We think the Wright Isle is a wonderful idea," Maeve said. "We're glad Cynthia suggested it."

What even my father didn't know was that Maeve and I had planned on the Wright Isle Resort all along.

"As it happens, I've discussed the idea with the hotel manager. He assures me the facility will be available, and the hotel staff will work to make it a most memorable event."

Maeve shook her head, and her lips curled into a crooked smile. "I hate it when he talks like that. What he means is, we've already talked to Hernando, who said it will be no problem, and we'll all have a great time."

Giving her an exaggerated pout, I asked, "Isn't that what I just said?"

"Not in so many words, dear," Maeve said. "Now hush."

My father put his hands on the table and rose to his feet. "I think this is the time in the wedding plan discussions when the men excuse themselves and the ladies take over. I'm sure they'll let us know what we need to do, and when. Ladies, may we be excused?"

My mother responded. "That is a capital idea, Owen. You men should all go for a walk in the river."

"Don't you mean a walk by the river, Mrs. Lanier?"

Derrick asked.

"Suit yourselves," my mom said with a shrug.

With that, the men were dismissed. The ladies got down to business planning the wedding.

Derrick asked if I thought I should be more involved in the preparations. Ted and my father enjoyed taking turns informing Derrick that the groom has only one role in a wedding: to show up. All the rest is for the mothers, the bride, and the bridal party, in that order.

I would, as the groom, get to propose a list of groomsmen subject to the bride's approval. And I got to choose my Best Man.

On that note, Derrick asked if the dads minded if he and I talked alone for a minute. They offered to wait on the porch and join us on the dock later. Derrick and I went for a walk.

As we made our way along the road, Derrick turned to me. "Mike, I want you to know that if you wanted me to be your Best Man, I would've loved to do it. But I know you and Hans have been best friends for a long time."

Derrick's choice of words struck me as odd. "Okay. Thanks for letting me off the hook on that. I was trying to figure out how to tell you I already asked Hans. Now, what do you mean 'would have loved to?' I don't like how that sounds. You are going to be at the wedding." I said this as a statement, not a question.

"That's what I need to talk to you about," Derrick said, his brow furrowing. "How can I tell you this?" He bit his lip and looked at the ground. Then he raised his head and blurted out, "Mike, I joined the Marines."

I choked back a laugh. Derrick didn't look like he was joking.

"The Marines! You joined the Marines. Were you going to mention this? When did this happen?"

"Remember the job I got at the martial arts studio?" Derrick asked.

"Yes," I replied cautiously.

"One of the regulars is the Marine Corps recruiter. He and I got to talking. Sergeant Everhart explained how, by enlisting in the Marine Corps Reserve, I could earn money for school, attend the Platoon Leader Course, and graduate college with a commission in the Corps."

I was relieved to hear that the plan included finishing college. "So you're not actually about to ship out to boot camp on your way to join the fleet?"

Derrick's face tightened, and his stance grew tense. "Mike, I know you were in the Navy. But the Marines are offering me a great opportunity."

I realized he thought I was knocking the Marine Corps. "Derrick, I have a lot of respect for the Marines. Both my grandfathers served in the Corps. My Grandpa Rollings fought as a Marine in France. My Grandpa Lanier got over there right at the end of the war. And my dad was in the Navy during Korea. I saw ... well, never mind that. I guess I'm just surprised, that's all."

His face softened, and his body relaxed. He looked down at his shoes. "I'm sorry, man. I never knew all that. I guess I knew your dad was a vet, but not about your granddads. You've never really talked about what you did in the Navy or anything. Then, the way you said that about shipping out."

I reached out and put a hand on his shoulder. "I was just surprised. This kinda came out of left field. If it's a Reserve thing, why do you have to miss the wedding?"

Derrick looked up and explained. "Boot camp starts right after we get out of school in May and goes for eleven weeks. I'll get done just in time to visit home before coming back to school."

"Have you told your folks about this?" I asked.

"Dad's cool with it. My mom isn't thrilled."

"What does Cynthia think?"

Derrick looked puzzled. "Why would I tell Cynthia?"

"Aren't you two ... I thought you two really hit it off," I said.

Derrick shook his head and then laughed. "Nah, man, it's not like that. I mean, I like her, and she is nice looking, but dude, she's much older than me. Cynthia is a nice lady, but it's not like you're thinking. We're just friends."

Maeve and I had really gotten the wrong impression. Wanting to change the subject, I asked, "By the way, did you know my Uncle Tim was in the Marines, too? He's a retired fighter pilot."

"No, man, I didn't know that. That is so cool," Derrick said. Then he became serious. "How come you never talk about what you did in the Navy?"

I didn't feel it was the right time to go into

that. Shrugging, I said, "I drove little boats, nothing exciting."

"Well, hey, at least you served. Now we'll have that in common."

"Just don't expect me to salute you," I said.

CHAPTER TWENTY-FIVE

November 1983

We turned and walked back to the dock. My father was telling Ted about my boats. I wondered just how much Ted understood about how well-heeled I was. Maybe my father had explained it to him. I knew Ted must have some idea.

Then another thought hit me. Had Maeve told them about the Nadeau's house? What did they think of that? They hadn't mentioned it. I needed to ask Maeve about that.

As Derrick and I joined them, Ted turned to me. "Has Maeve told you about my Flying Scott?"

"She has," I said. "Don't you miss it?"

With a sad smile, Ted said, "Only when there's a light breeze on a warm day."

"You're welcome to come up and take *Riverscape*

out any time you want."

"I may take you up on that," Ted said. The look on his face struck a chord with me. "She's a nice little boat. How about the Hunter? Do you get much chance to sail her?"

"I'm ashamed to say she's not seen the water since summer. Hopefully, that will be rectified next year. Maeve and I are going to sail her on our honeymoon."

The news seemed to surprise my dad. "Are you? Where are you planning to go?"

I outlined our plan. "We want to go down the coast to Florida, and then over to the Bahamas. If we feel confident enough by then, we'll sail open water directly back here from the islands."

"Are you certified for ocean passage?" Ted asked.

"I am. Next spring, Maeve wants to take some classes so she can be too."

"That sounds like something I'd like to do someday," Ted said. "I do miss sailing."

An idea hit me. "How long are you going to hang around tomorrow?"

"Most of the day, I imagine," Ted said. "Now that you two have set a date, the ladies will plan and plan every spare minute until the day of."

"Then let's go sailing," I suggested. "Sure, it'll be cold, but I've got some gear you can wear. Derrick, Dad, and I were going to sail *Riverscape* up to Oriental for winter storage tomorrow. You can join the crew. The Mariner 19 is enough like a Scott size-wise that you'll be shipshape in no time."

Ted's eyes lit up like he'd just won a prize. "I'd like

that."

That settled, we decided it was getting too cold to stand around out on the dock and headed back to the house. Upon walking in, we noticed the ladies had quit the dining room in favor of the comforts of the living room, including the woodstove. I noticed Cynthia wasn't there.

"Did Cynthia head back to camp?" I asked.

"No," called a voice from the kitchen. "I'm out here sneaking another piece of cake."

Maeve laughed and then called back, "You know it's not really sneaking if you tell everyone about it."

"I suppose not," we heard Cynthia say. "Would anybody else like some?"

We all decided we'd like some. I volunteered to go into the kitchen and help Cynthia. That earned me a few odd looks, but Maeve nodded approvingly.

"I suppose you want a piece," Cynthia said when she saw me walk into the kitchen.

"Yes, I do," I said. "But I actually came to help. You slice the cake, I'll scoop the ice cream, and I'll dragoon Derrick to deliver."

Cynthia decided it was time to clear up the misconception about her and Derrick. "Mike, your friend Derrick's cute, and a nice kid, but I think you've gotten the wrong idea."

"I did, but now I don't. Derrick already clarified for me."

"If he were a few years older, maybe, or I were a few years younger, who knows," Cynthia said as she placed a slice of cake on the plate I held out to her.

Digging the scoop into the ice cream, I teased, "It's a shame really. You two make a cute couple."

"Michael, you brat," Maeve said, having heard only the last part of my remark. "Has Cynthia straightened you out about Derrick?"

Cynthia answered before I could. "I was going to, but Derrick already did."

"Did Cynthia tell you I've asked her to be my maid of honor?" Maeve asked.

Cynthia shook her head as she cut another slice of cake. "No, I haven't told him that yet. Now I don't have to. You just did."

Unable to stop myself, I said, "I'll bet Maeve took it pretty hard when you told her you'd rather eat a bug."

That earned me a simultaneous "Brat!" in stereo. Then we all broke out laughing.

"We're all out there waiting for cake, and you guys are in here laughing it up," Derrick said as he strode into the kitchen, hands on his hips. "How about some service around this place?"

The parents had sent him in to see what was taking so long.

"I'll give you service," Cynthia said. She smeared his nose with frosting. Before he could retaliate, Maeve handed him a plate and told him to take it to her mom.

Soon, with no more frosted noses, we were all sitting around the living room - over-30s on the seats, under-30s on the floor - eating cake and discussing the virtues of lilies over roses as a choice for the bouquet. The ladies were discussing the bouquet. We men were just sitting there enjoying our cake.

From somewhere, several issues of *Brides* magazine appeared. When I asked about this, no one would claim credit or acknowledge guilt, depending on your perspective. Eventually, everyone grew weary enough to decide it was time to head to our respective sleeping quarters for the night.

Once we were alone in our bedroom, Maeve said, "I guess we jumped to the wrong conclusion about Derrick and Cynthia."

I laughed, thinking about it. "I'd say we did."

"What's this about Dad going sailing with you tomorrow? I thought you guys were just going to motor up to your launch ramp and trailer to the marina."

"We were. But when I saw the wistful look in your father's eye when he started talking about sailing, I decided, what the heck. I figured you ladies would be busy with wedding details and wouldn't miss us."

Maeve gave me one of those *oh please* looks over her shoulder. Then she turned around. "Speaking of wedding details, did you ask Hans to be your Best Man before he left today?"

"Yes, I did," I said. "He said he would be honored and asked if I wanted regular strippers for my bachelor party, or perhaps ladies from some exotic locale." Hans really asked me that.

"You tell him they had better be the invisible kind," Maeve said. Judging from the way her lips were pressed into a tight, thin line, it was a good thing I'd told Hans no strippers.

After staring at me long enough to be sure I'd gotten the message, she asked, "Did you tell Derrick?"

I sat on the edge of the bed and reached out to take her hand. "Funny thing about that. Derrick told me before I could bring it up and ask him to be a groomsman. He told me I should ask Hans to be my Best Man."

Maeve sat down beside me and softly laid her hand on the back of my neck. "He knows you and Hans have been best friends since forever. He probably figured you'd want to ask Hans and decided to let you off the hook."

"Well, there was that," I said. "And the fact that he won't be able to make the wedding."

I cringed, waiting for her reaction.

Maeve sat up straight, her eyes narrowing. "WHAT!?!"

She reacted just as I expected. "Derrick won't be at the wedding. He joined the Marines. He said when your sister broke his heart, it was either that or the foreign legion."

Maeve stood, hands on hips, and glared at me. "This isn't funny. Why can't he be at the wedding?"

My attempt at deflecting her with humor having failed, I told her the facts. "You're right. It has nothing to do with Cynthia. Derrick joined the Marine Corps Reserve. He leaves for boot camp right after the spring semester ends."

Maeve wagged a finger in my face. "Well then, he'll just have to tell the Marines they'll have to wait."

"Sweetheart, he can't do that. His schedule's

confirmed. He has to go then in order to be back in time for school in the fall."

Her shoulders slumped, and she shook her head. Her mouth twisted into a frown. "So, he only joined the Marines for the summer?"

"He joined the Marine Corps Reserve," I said. "It's part of a process that ends up with him being commissioned as a second lieutenant when he graduates."

Maeve plopped down on the bed next to me. Hearing that didn't make her like it any better. "He's got a lot of nerve."

"Babe, he didn't do it just to get out of being in the wedding. He feels terrible about it. He did it because they'll help him pay for school, and he'll get a head start on a career."

"You could have helped him pay for school," she snapped, and then realized what she'd said. "No, I'm sorry. I shouldn't have said that."

I sighed. "I thought of that. Derrick would never accept it from me. Knowing that, I wouldn't offend his pride by offering. It's a shame, really. His parents are helping him out as much as they can, and he got some scholarship money, but he still comes up short. He got a part-time job a few weeks ago, and now he's gone and joined the Marines."

"It is hard for most people. I'm going to be years paying off student loans," Maeve said.

"What about the money your grandmother left you?"

"My year at Yale ate most of that up. There was

enough left over to cover room and board for the last three years, but I had to borrow money for tuition and stuff. When I go to work, I've got to start paying it off."

That Maeve had student loans hadn't occurred to me. "You don't have to worry about them anymore."

She pulled away and lowered her chin. "What do you mean?"

"Now that I know about them, I'll take care of them."

"I don't expect you to do that," Maeve whispered.

I reached out and pulled her closer. "I know you don't. If you did, I probably wouldn't."

She put her arms around my neck and kissed my cheek. "I suppose that makes some kind of sense. Still, I wish there was some way you could help Derrick."

"I have. But I could only do so much without him figuring it out. He's about to receive a letter telling him that he has received a housing allowance for next year from the little-known Children of Injured Law Officers Benevolent Fund. It will explain that he became eligible when the fund learned of his dad's injury in the line of duty."

Maeve's eyebrows rose. "Won't he see through that?"

"If he calls the number, he'll find out it's a real charity. As long as he doesn't ask how long they've been around, or how many other cops' kids they've helped, it'll be fine."

"Isn't that kind of underhanded?" Maeve asked.

"Not really. It's a real charity. I contacted some people I know after Derrick's dad got hurt and told them I wanted to set up a fund to help injured cops' kids pay for college, and that I wanted Derrick to be the first recipient. It's even registered with the IRS, and people can donate to it."

Maeve smiled and shook her head. "Just like that. You created a charity out of thin air to help a friend. You are amazing."

The tender way she said it nearly made me blush. "Sometimes, when you have more money than sense, you have to be careful how you use it. You don't want to look like you're, I don't know, bragging or something. That's why whenever I want to help out somewhere, I try to stay out of the picture."

"So now I know who you really are," Maeve said. "You're the world-famous Anonymous Donor." She laughed but stopped when she saw the look on my face. "Mike, what?"

How could I explain? "Maeve, even when I want to, I can't just go paying everyone's way. If I did, the people I hang out with wouldn't want to hang out with me, and the people who would want to hang out with me wouldn't be people I want to hang out with. Do you see?"

Maeve looked at me for a very long time. "Mike, I'm sorry. I never thought about it like that. To me, you're just my Michael, and I love you. Derrick and Hans - you're just their buddy Mike. Sure, they know you've got more stuff than the average guy, but so what? They like you, not your stuff. You've worked hard, and your parents did, too, so all that wealth wouldn't mess you up. And it worked. You're the most squared-away guy I've ever known. You've got a big heart and a clear head. I'm very lucky I found you, so very lucky."

Hugging her to me, I said, "Maeve, you're the best thing that's ever happened to me. I'm the lucky one. You're so complete and confident in who you are. So strong, yet so tender. You don't need me, but I am only complete because you're with me."

"No, Mike, you're wrong about that. I'm only complete because being with you makes me complete. We're two halves of a whole, Michael, soul mates."

"I love you so much, Maeve Dalton Lanier," I said, my heart nearly bursting.

"I love you, Michael, I love you so very much." Nothing more needed to be said.

CHAPTER
TWENTY-SIX

November 1983

We rose before the sun, smiling and happy. Maeve and I had reached a new level in our relationship the night before. We'd grown together as a couple and learned a greater level of trust and understanding. Now we rose to face the world, a stronger force to be reckoned with than we were the day before.

It was a chilly morning, not yet forty degrees out. Maeve and I went to the kitchen, got a pot of coffee going, and started breakfast. We planned to surprise my parents with eggs to order.

Maeve started some biscuits baking. The kind that comes in a tube from the refrigerator. I went to the living room and fired up the woodstove. I made enough noise to wake my folks without making it obvious that's what I was doing. By the time I headed back to the kitchen, I heard them stirring.

My father got to the kitchen first. He headed straight for the coffeepot.

"So, Michael," he said as he filled his mug, "are you sure you want to sail to Oriental this morning? I thought we were just going to motor over to your ramp and trailer the boat to Jeremy's."

"That's what I asked him last night, Dad," Maeve said, giving me an I-told-you-so look.

I took a sip of coffee. Then I explained why I'd changed my mind. "I thought that since the ladies will probably spend all day talking about the wedding, we men might as well make a day of it. Besides, did you see Ted's eyes when he talked about sailing? How could I not offer?"

That was good enough for my dad. "It's going to be awfully cold on the water. I hope we can all stay dry."

"Who needs to stay dry?" my mom asked when she walked into the kitchen.

"The menfolk are going sailing while we womenfolk spend the day talking about gowns and flowers and such," Maeve said, affecting a delightful, if somewhat over-the-top, southern belle accent.

"Oh, I see," my mother said.

I could tell by the look on Maeve's face that she thought my mom would have more to say on the subject. But before she could, Ted and Phyllis let themselves in.

Ted was practically bouncing as he walked in. "Good morning, everybody. It looks like a brisk morning for a sail."

I looked at Maeve and mouthed, told-you-so. She stuck her tongue out at me.

"At least you need to get some breakfast first. Dad, you like yours over easy, right?" Maeve said.

"That would be great, Maeve, thanks," Ted said. "Mike, you said you had some warm gear you thought would fit."

"I sure do, Ted. It's down in a locker on *Geddaway*. I'll get it while you have breakfast."

My mother stopped me before I could get to the door. "You need a good breakfast, too, young man, if you are going sailing in this weather."

"I agree. You can wait to get those things after you've eaten," Phyllis said.

Now, I might argue with my mother, or with my mother-in-law, but I wasn't crazy enough to argue with my mother and mother-in-law when they agreed on an issue.

"Yes'm, yes'm, I'll eat my breakfast first," I said, bowing to each of them meekly.

"By the way, dear, how do you plan to get home after you drop off the boat at Jeremy's?" Maeve asked.

Taking a seat at the table, I said, "That does seem to be one detail I overlooked."

Maeve's annoyed look reminded me I was supposed to be helping her cook breakfast.

There was another knock on the door, and in walked Derrick and Cynthia. I wondered if we'd have enough eggs.

Cynthia arrived with the solution to the dilemma Maeve had just presented to me.

"Maeve, I have a brilliant idea. Why don't we drive into Oriental this morning so we can look around town? Then we'll meet the men for lunch at the end of their voyage. Derrick was just telling me they'll need a ride back."

"That's an excellent idea," Maeve said.

She handed Cynthia a coffee cup and raised a questioning eyebrow at Derrick. He nodded, and she filled him a cup.

Rising to fulfill my duties at the stove, I said, "It is as long as someone drives Dad's Suburban. We'll need it to haul back any gear we don't want to leave on the boat."

"I'll drive the Suburban," my mom said as she took the seat I'd just vacated.

"I'll take my car," Cynthia said. "That way we'll have room for everybody and the gear on the way back." She refilled her coffee cup and held the pot out for Derrick.

Cracking eggs into a bowl, I said, "Well, that problem was easily solved."

"No thanks to you," Maeve said, and then laughed.

After breakfast, my intrepid crew and I set out to rig *Riverscape* for its last sail of the season. The sun was up just enough to warm things. The forecast was for light winds and a high temperature of sixty.

I gingerly climbed aboard *Geddaway*, up on its lift, and retrieved foul weather gear for Ted and Derrick. Suitably attired, we'd have no problems on this cruise. The Mariner was a very stable boat, and the winds were light. The problem would've been not having enough speed. In that case, there was always the auxiliary outboard.

By the time we were geared up, the sun was up enough to sail by. I showed off a little by leaving the dock under sail. We moved so slowly at first that I heard Cynthia wonder aloud if we were becalmed. Then the jib caught the wind and moved the bow away from the dock.

As the mainsail fluttered, I trimmed the sail and pushed the tiller over. Shortly, we were sailing smartly away from the dock towards the center of the river. The winds were west-northwest. I set us on a broad reach towards a point in the middle of the river halfway between Oriental and Cedar Creek.

Once we were underway, I offered Ted the tiller and pointed out the landmark to make for. His smile when he took hold of the tiller made me glad I'd decided to sail *Riverscape* to Oriental.

Since they weren't needed topside once we were underway, Derrick and my dad retreated to the small cabin with a thermos of coffee. I remained with Ted in the cockpit to answer questions he might have about the boat, to man the jib sheets should it be needed, and just to talk.

Ted adjusted the mainsheet as the wind picked up a notch.

"She's a nice boat, Mike. She feels good in the water."

"Thanks, Ted. I enjoy her. I just don't get her out here as often as she deserves," I said. "Maybe this spring you and Phyllis can come down and take her out once in a while."

"I'd like that. Phyllis would too. She loved sailing on the Scott."

We sailed along in silence for a few minutes. Derrick poked his head up from the cabin and gave us cups of coffee. Ted cleated the mainsheet and sipped gingerly at his.

"Mike, you know Phyllis and I like you very much, don't you?"

I tasted my coffee before replying. "I hoped so. Thanks, Ted, for telling me. I think the world of both of you."

"I have to say this, Mike, as her father. I love my little girl. She's my baby. I wasn't crazy at first with the idea of you two getting engaged. You'd barely known each other a month."

Before I could remind him we'd known each other longer than that, Ted said, "No, let me finish, Mike. I know you worked at camp together for a couple of years. That was when you were just kids."

He paused and seemed to gather his thoughts.

"I wasn't crazy about it. Shoot, I was upset about it. Then, you two came to the house, and I saw you together. I saw how happy you made her. I saw how much you purely loved Maeve, and how much she loved you.

"That's when it hit me. You two were as joined as you could ever be. No words from a preacher or paperwork from the county office could improve on that. So, I not only accepted your being engaged, I came to embrace it.

"I tried to explain it to Phyllis. She wondered why it had taken me so long to see it. She saw it right off. I think she knew from talking to Maeve before the first time you ever came to our house. Then you two surprised me again by going ahead and getting married, instead of living together like so many do these days. I knew then that as a father, I couldn't ask more of a son-in-law. I knew you would take good care of my little girl.

"What I guess I'm trying to say, Mike, is that while we're looking forward to the wedding as a celebration of the love between you and Maeve, Phyllis and I know in our hearts that it's not just a marriage because of a piece of paper from the county office. In your spirits, in your souls, you are truly joined."

I wasn't sure what to say, so for a few minutes I said nothing. We just sailed on, enjoying the sound of the wind in the rigging and the water moving past the hull. Finally, I found my voice.

"Ted, I love Maeve very much. I wasn't a whole person until she became a part of my life. I can't imagine having to ever be without her. I'll do everything in my power to keep her safe, to make her happy, and most of all, to let her know she is loved every second of every day."

Now it was Ted's turn to digest what I'd said. "Michael, a father can't ask more from the man who married his daughter. I know you don't need it and haven't asked for it. It's kind of old-fashioned to even talk about it. But, son, you have my blessing."

I felt a swell of pride. "Thank you, Ted. That means

more to me than I can say. Thank you."

It was cold out on the river that morning. After a few more minutes, Ted and I agreed it was time for a shift change. Derrick and my dad came out to take over. Ted and I eased into the cabin to warm up some. I learned a lot about my father-in-law on that cruise.

Ted was born and raised in Lumberton. After high school, he did a tour in the Army as a signalman, where he developed an interest in communications technologies. He used his GI Bill to go to school at North Carolina State, where he earned his degree as an electrical engineer. It was at State that he met Phyllis. They married within days of his graduation. His first job was with a company in Southport. He and Phyllis moved there, and a year later Cynthia was born. Three and a half years after that, Maeve came along.

Ted's company moved him to Whiteville near the end of Cynthia's senior year of high school, which was Maeve's freshman year. Phyllis and the girls stayed in Southport through the end of the school year so Cynthia could graduate with her high school class. Cynthia went to the NC State School of Engineering on scholarships, earned partly on her math skills and partly on her volleyball skills. That Cynthia was fit was something you couldn't miss, but I hadn't pictured her as an athlete.

"I had no idea Cynthia played sports at school."

"Oh, yes," said Ted, with a proud smile. "She played all through high school and college."

Three years after they moved to Whiteville, Maeve graduated from high school and left home for her glorious tenure at Yale. Deciding Yale wasn't her glass of sweet tea, she came home to attend UNCW. The money from her grandmother was mostly used up by then. She earned some scholarships that helped pay tuition and took out student loans to pay for room and board. Neither girl would let her parents put themselves in hock for her college.

Ted looked down at his hands as he said, "Phyllis and I never put any money aside for their college. Foolish of us, I suppose. We always figured on taking out a second mortgage on the house or something. The girls wouldn't hear of it. Their inheritance from Phyllis's mom helped. They each paid their own way. We helped as much as they'd let us, of course. I'm very proud of them, though, for doing it on their own."

Ted told me Maeve couldn't decide whether to major in English or Education. She did both.

"It meant a lot of extra courses for her. She's taken classes every winter session and every summer. In her first two years, she took eighteen credit hours a semester. Then, in the fall of her junior year, she spent a semester studying abroad in Spain."

I remembered Maeve mentioning her semester in Spain, but I hadn't thought much about it at the time. Now, it gave me an idea. "Ted, do you think Maeve would like to go back to Spain?"

Ted's brow creased, and he closed one eye. "I know she liked it over there. Sure, she'd probably like to go back. Why?"

We switched off again. Derrick and Dad returned to the cabin to warm up. The sun was higher in the sky and the air warmer, but it remained chilly out on the water. At least we were sailing with the wind, so the wind chill wasn't as bad as it might have been if we'd been sailing to weather.

Picking up our conversation where we'd left off, I said, "I just had a thought about the honeymoon. Maybe instead of the Bahamas, Maeve and I could cruise the coast of Spain?"

Ted, eyebrows scrunched, looked at me out of the corner of his eye. "Would you be able to sail that Hunter of yours across to Spain?"

"Maybe. Probably. But we wouldn't do it that way. I was thinking we'd fly over and pick up a bareboat charter in Cadiz or Gibraltar. Then we could sail east along the coast."

"Sounds like an enjoyable trip. Maeve would like that," Ted said.

I checked my watch and our location against the chart. By my calculations, it was time to turn towards Oriental. Ted offered the tiller, but I asked him to remain there while I handled the jib. He smiled and sat up higher on the rail.

I let the guys in the cabin know we were preparing to tack and then told Ted to give the command when he was ready. He made the move like an old pro. We trimmed up and headed back across the river.

After one more change of the watch, we all returned to the cockpit. I decided we should motor into the marina rather than try to maneuver in under sail. No one thought it was a bad idea. Though we appeared to be the only boat underway, it was still a rather narrow approach to the ramp where Jeremy would lift *Riverscape* out.

Being a Sunday, and a holiday weekend besides, *Riverscape* would remain tied up at the dock until Tuesday. Dick, Jeremy's assistant manager, was on duty. He said he'd call me down in Wilmington once they had her out, winterized, and put away for the season. We'd no sooner finished offloading the gear I didn't want to leave on board than the ladies arrived.

"It appears you all arrived warm, dry, and in one piece," my mother said.

"In one piece, anyway," my father quipped.

"Warm is a relative term," Derrick pointed out. "I feel a lot warmer now than I did after twenty minutes at the helm."

"I'm just glad you're all here safe and sound," Maeve said. "Now, let's go get some lunch."

We loaded up my dad's truck with the gear from the boat, piled into the vehicles, and headed out to find some lunch. We wound up at Scooba's for pizza. It wasn't Dupree's, but it was the best in Pamlico County. After putting away a couple of Scooba's best, it was back to the house and time for goodbyes. We encouraged everyone to take home some of the barbeque. By the time they were all gone, it was too.

Relaxing onto the couch with relief, I asked Maeve, "Do you hear that?"

Maeve cocked her head and gave me a quizzical frown. "I don't hear anything," she said before sitting down beside me.

I sighed. "I know. Isn't it great?"

She smacked me none too gently on the shoulder. "Michael, they were here to celebrate with you."

Properly chastised, I said, "I know. I had a great time. The pig picking was a blast. I really enjoyed it. Now, I'm ready to enjoy some time here alone with you."

Maeve leaned back and rested her head on my shoulder. "I'll admit it. As much as I liked having everyone here, I'm glad we've still got tonight and tomorrow all to ourselves."

CHAPTER TWENTY-SEVEN

November 1983

Since everyone left on Sunday, Maeve and I were on our own on Monday. We spent the day at River Dream, relaxing and discussing honeymoon ideas.

"When we were sailing *Riverscape* to Oriental, I came up with another idea for our honeymoon destination."

Maeve arched an eyebrow. Her lips twitched with a hint of a grin. "Oh, you did, did you?"

My lips curved into a smile. "Yes, I did, did I. I was wondering if you might like to move our cruise a little farther to the east."

It was late afternoon. We were sitting on the porch looking out over the river. Maeve rocked back in her wicker rocker, folded her hands in her lap, and eyed me suspiciously.

"Just how far east are we talking about here? The Turks and Caicos, Puerto Rico?"

I shook my head, and my smile widened. "Farther."

Her eyes narrowed as she tried to picture a map of the Caribbean. "Antigua, Martinique?"

Still shaking my head, I chuckled. Maeve frowned and grasped the arms of her rocker.

"Where then? There's not much east of Martinique."

My rocker creaked as I leaned back and stretched my arms. "You have to go about three thousand miles farther east," I said.

Maeve's eyes grew wide, and she sat up straight in her chair. "Are you talking about sailing to Europe? I don't think so, Mike. Could *Geddaway* even make it there?"

I let her off the hook and explained. "We wouldn't sail from here to there. I was thinking we'd fly to Gibraltar, charter a boat, and then spend a few weeks sailing up the coast of Spain. Your dad reminded me of the time you spent in Spain last year. I thought you might enjoy going back."

Her blue eyes sparkled, and her pursed lips relaxed into a smile.

"Can I take that smile to mean you like the idea?"

Maeve gave an exaggerated nod. "Yes, Michael, you can take this smile to mean I like the idea."

CHAPTER TWENTY-EIGHT

The Holidays 1983

Planning the wedding was in the hands of Maeve and our moms. Planning the honeymoon was left to me. With help from the fine folks at Wilmington to the World Travel, I worked out most of the details before Thanksgiving.

Just where Maeve and I were going to spend our first Thanksgiving as a married couple was the subject of much discussion. We wound up having Thanksgiving dinner with my folks the Wednesday night before. On Thanksgiving Day, we drove to Whiteville for dinner with Maeve's folks. We drove to Tuscarora on Friday for dinner with Grandma Lillian and my Aunt Donna's family. On Friday evening we drove the rest of the way to River Dream and spent the weekend alone at home.

We were still staying at Maeve's college apartment by Thanksgiving when we were in Wilmington. Maeve and Kim's lease went through August. As luck would have it, University Arms was not part of the Coastal Carolina Realty Trust, so I couldn't tweak the lease.

What I could do, and what I did, was front Kim Maeve's share of the rent so she would have plenty of time to find a new roommate. Maeve and I moved into the house on Wrightsville Beach a few days before Christmas.

After all the miles we logged getting around at Thanksgiving, Maeve and I thought it would be nice if everyone came to see us for Christmas. Being we'd just moved in; this was of a challenge. With help from my folks, who lived just down the island, and the excellent service provided by the delivery department at several local stores, we were furnished, decorated, and ready to entertain on Christmas Day.

The Nadeaus, in exchange for being able to stay in the house after closing, worked with us to get the painting and flooring done before they moved out. The kitchen appliances had been replaced a week before they left, with their fridge, washer, and dryer going into storage.

I suggested having dinner catered. Maeve and her mom got on the phone to Cynthia, my mom, and Grandma Lillian. They decided on a potluck.

Maeve and I bought a Christmas tree at the Optimist Club lot. It was a big Douglas fir. I wasn't sure it was going to fit in our living room, but it did, with only inches to spare.

Maeve had a box of ornaments from her mother. Each Christmas, Phyllis and Ted gave the girls new ornaments. Phyllis saved them over the years. On her first Christmas in her own house, Phyllis gave Maeve hers.

"Mike, did your family have any holiday traditions like that?" Maeve asked as she looked through the box of mementos from her Christmases past.

I stopped arranging the lights on the tree long enough to answer her. "When I was little, we'd go over to Grandma and Grandpa Lanier's every Christmas Eve for a big family gathering. It got to be quite a crowd when everyone was there - us, my Aunt Donna with her husband and my cousin Denise, Uncle Gary with his wife and kids, and Uncle Chris."

Looking up from her ornaments, Maeve rubbed her chin and asked, "Why don't y'all do that anymore?"

"After Grandpa passed away and Grandma moved, those gatherings sort of withered."

A stab of nostalgia brought a wistful smile to my face. I shook it off and went on hanging lights on the tree.

We spent most of the day before Christmas cleaning the house and rearranging furniture. Maeve and I, worn out by our preparations for Christmas Day, stayed home and watched *It's a Wonderful Life* on cable Christmas Eve. We fell asleep on the couch, woke up enough to turn off the television, and were headed to bed when there came a noise out on the street. It sounded like a car pulling up in front of the house.

"Mike, shouldn't you go take a look?" Maeve asked nervously.

Pretty sure I knew what it was, I couldn't help but pick on her a bit. "I suppose I should. Let me grab my shotgun."

With an exasperated frown, Maeve said, "You don't have a shotgun. Just go take a look out the window."

I walked over to the window and looked out. There by the street sat a red 1984 Porsche 944 wrapped with an enormous bow and a large card that said *Merry Christmas, Maeve.*

"Well, what is it?" Maeve asked.

Working hard to keep a straight face, I said, "It looks like Santa making an early delivery."

"Seriously, Michael, what is it?" Maeve said. She sounded like she was getting annoyed.

"Let's go down and take a look," I said.

"I'll just come and look out the window for myself, geez," Maeve said. She looked out the window, spotted the car, read the tag, and drew in a breath.

"Michael ..."

Stepping back and holding up my hands, I denied responsibility.

"Don't look at me. Blame the guy in the red suit with the white beard who parked it there."

Maeve grabbed my hand and practically dragged me downstairs and outside to the car.

"Michael! It's exactly the one I wanted - red with tan leather seats. How? When? Oh, Mike, I love it."

She was smiling like a kid who'd just found a pony

under the tree Christmas morning.

"Shall we take it for a drive?" I asked.

Maeve threw her arms around my neck, practically knocking me off my feet.

"Of course we should. Uh, where are the keys?"

I told her the keys were inside under the visor as I removed the bow and card. After tossing them in back, we climbed in. Maeve checked out every button and switch before starting it up and getting turned around.

Finally, we were on our way down the road on a Christmas Eve midnight ride. We drove down and around the South End. We drove up to the North End. Then we drove home, and Maeve pulled the Porsche into the driveway.

"Oh, Michael, I love it. It drives so nice. Thank you, sweetheart."

I leaned over the center console, reached up, gently touched her cheek, kissed her lightly, and said, "Merry Christmas, baby."

Maeve insisted we move her old Corolla out of the garage and put the Porsche in. For just a moment, when I moved her old car out, she looked at it wistfully. Then she looked at the new car and smiled.

"That old Toyota was a good car. In a funny way, I'm going to miss it."

"We'll find it a good home," I said.

"Yeah, maybe we could put it out to pasture where it could run free with all the other old cars." Maeve laughed at her own joke and said, "We'll just sell it. It's just a car after all."

She climbed back into the 944 and carefully pulled it into the garage.

Holding the door for her as she got out, I said, "Let's get to bed, babe. We've got a busy day tomorrow."

Giving the Porsche a gentle pat on the fender, she led me upstairs to the bedroom.

CHAPTER TWENTY-NINE

Christmas 1983

At seven o'clock on Christmas morning, we were awakened by a knock on the door. I pulled on a pair of gym shorts and trudged through the house to see who had interrupted my much-needed rest. It was Cynthia.

"Don't just stand there, Michael. There's a box in the car I need you to bring in."

"Good morning to you, too, Cynthia," I said. "Merry Christmas."

That's how the day began, with me going out to Cynthia's car in my gym shorts and T-shirt to retrieve whatever was in the box. It was cold. The forecast was for cold and clear. The cold was definitely correct. The thermometer by the garage door showed 28 degrees. I was shivering by the time I got back inside with the box.

"Bring it to the kitchen, Michael," Cynthia called out. "I'll need it in here."

After setting the box on the kitchen table, I asked, "What is all this for?"

"The ingredients I need for my cheesecake, along with the springboard pan and mixer," Cynthia said as she began removing items from the box.

I perked up at the word cheesecake.

"In that case, I forgive you for waking me up at this hour and making me trudge half-naked through the cold to retrieve it."

"Good morning, Cynthia. Merry Christmas," Maeve said as she came into the kitchen. "What have you been making Michael trudge through the cold for?"

"Good morning, Sis. Merry Christmas," Cynthia said. "I asked whiny boy over there to bring in a box full of things I need to make my cheesecake."

"Your cheesecake? Your special Christmas cheesecake?" Maeve asked, clearly excited by the prospect.

"Yes, my special Christmas cheesecake," Cynthia answered, carefully enunciating every word.

"In that case, I forgive you for making him go out in the cold to get the box," Maeve said.

"So, what's all this about a special Christmas cheesecake?" I asked. The girls looked at each other and laughed.

"Cynthia invented a secret cheesecake recipe that she only makes for Christmas," Maeve said. "She won't let anyone watch while she mixes it. It is ambrosia."

"Well, I don't claim it's that good. But everyone does seem to like it," Cynthia said. She checked each item as she set it on the counter.

My curiosity had been piqued. "You've never given anyone the recipe?"

Cynthia, without looking up from her task, shook her head. "Nope. So, what were you guys still doing in bed? Or shouldn't I ask?"

Stifling a yawn, I said, "Actually, we were asleep. We were up rather late trying out Maeve's present from Santa."

"Oh, really? And what might that be?" Cynthia asked.

"It's in the garage. Come see it before you get started," Maeve said.

Cynthia and Maeve went down to the garage so Maeve could show off her present. Several minutes later, they returned.

Cynthia was impressed. "Michael, that's a very nice present."

"I can't believe Santa actually brought it for her," I said. "How in the world did he get it on his sleigh?"

"Elvin magic, I suppose," Maeve said, smiling.

Cynthia chuckled and rolled her eyes. "That would explain it. Now, you two need to do whatever you need to do in the kitchen and then get out so I can get to work."

"You're in luck. Maeve and I don't need to do anything in the kitchen. We're expected for breakfast at my folks' house."

"We are?" Maeve asked, taken by surprise. "Oh,

yeah, we are. We'd better get dressed."

We left Cynthia in the kitchen and hurried back to the bedroom. I got on the phone and called my parents to explain why they had guests coming to breakfast. My dad answered the phone with, "Merry Christmas."

"Merry Christmas, Dad, I didn't wake you, did I?"

He gave a tired laugh. "It's Christmas morning. An almost twelve-year-old girl lives in this house. Do you really think you woke me up?"

An image of my sister Malori pacing outside my parents' bedroom door formed in my mind. "I guess not. Uh, what's for breakfast?"

"I don't know what you're having. I'm having waffles and sausage," my dad said.

"Would you have enough batter for two more?" I asked. "People, not waffles."

"I suppose I could," he said. "But why would I do that?"

I couldn't tell if he was truly annoyed about us coming to breakfast, or if he was just giving me a hard time for the fun of it.

"Cynthia just arrived and evicted Maeve and me from the kitchen. We haven't even had time to make a pot of coffee, much less breakfast."

When he replied, I could tell he was having a hard time not laughing out loud. "You were kicked out of your own kitchen on Christmas morning? You poor kids. I suppose I could save you a scrap or two. Of course, I'll fill a plate for Maeve. How long will it take you to get here?"

"We just need to get cleaned up and dressed, and

we'll be there. I'd say thirty minutes."

"Breakfast will probably be ready by then. Merry Christmas," my dad said.

I hung up the phone. We showered and got dressed. Saying goodbye to Cynthia, who was engrossed in her task in the kitchen, we headed down the island to my folks. We took the Porsche. Maeve wanted to show it off.

When we arrived at my mom and dad's, everyone wanted to come out and see Maeve's new car. Malori talked Maeve into taking her for a ride. Even my mother got a trip down around the South End before we headed inside for breakfast.

The waffles and sausage were staying warm in the oven. Malori was eager to show off what Santa brought her, but my mother insisted we eat first.

The ladies took seats while my dad and I served up breakfast. I poured myself a cup of coffee, and he handed me the maple syrup.

"You know, Dad, I wonder if we're the only people who sweeten their coffee with maple syrup."

He took the jug of syrup and added a healthy dollop to his own coffee. "I don't know, son. We're probably the only ones in New Hanover County. Maybe in North Carolina."

"Folks just don't know what they're missing," I said.

I sipped my coffee and was surprised. It was very, very good. Smooth and sweet, without a trace of bitterness.

"Wow, Dad, this is really excellent coffee. Where'd

you get it?"

"I made it myself," my dad said, grinning proudly. "Your mother bought me a coffee grinder for my birthday, and I've been experimenting with different beans. For this, I finely ground a half cup of dark roast Columbian beans and three large pieces of pecan. The pecans smooth out the bitterness. With the maple syrup, it makes a really nice flavor."

"You certainly stumbled onto something here. I'll have to get one of those coffee grinders."

I poured a cup for Maeve, and then we carried the plates with the waffles and sausage to the table.

"Wow! What kind of coffee it this? It's really good," Maeve said.

"It is Owen's own recipe," my mother said. "He has been trying different roasts and beans with his grinder. He finally found one he really likes."

"He uses pecans and maple syrup," Malori said. "He says it's a cross-cultural coffee - a little South American, a little southern, and a little northern."

"I'm glad everyone likes it." my dad said. "Now, can we get down to putting away some of these waffles?"

After breakfast, Malori showed off what we in the Lanier family called stocking presents. These were the presents left unwrapped under the tree along with the stocking. I don't think Malori still believed in Santa Claus when she was eleven, but if she didn't, she wasn't letting on.

Having given Malori a chance to show off her presents, Maeve called our house to see if Cynthia would let us back in. She got the all-clear, so we headed back after thanking my mom and dad for breakfast. They promised to be along directly.

Upon entering the house, the first thing that hit me was the enticing aroma of something wonderful baking. Then I heard the sound of White Christmas being played on a piano. It took me a minute to remember we had a piano.

"Did you leave the piano running?" I asked Maeve.

Maeve looked at me like I was a bit odd. "I imagine Cynthia's playing. She's quite good."

"I didn't know she played," I said.

Maeve nodded. "We both took lessons when we were kids. Hers stuck. Mine, not so much."

Cynthia must have heard us bantering. "Why don't you two come in here and get a fire going? Then I might let you sing along, if you can carry a tune."

"Let me run down to the garage to get my bucket," I said.

"What bucket?" Maeve asked.

"The bucket he needs to carry a tune," Cynthia answered for me, laughing.

"Nonsense, Mike. I've heard you sing. You're not half bad," Maeve said.

I curled my lips down in a frown and let my eyelids droop. "There is nothing like faint praise to boost the old ego."

While my wife and my sister-in-law shared a laugh at my expense, I went to the fireplace and got a small blaze going. Then we sang Christmas tunes until interrupted by a knock at the front door. It was Ted and Phyllis.

"Merry Christmas, Mom and Dad," Maeve greeted them.

"Merry Christmas, sweetheart," Phyllis said, giving her a hug.

"Merry Christmas to you both," Ted called out as he hugged her and then shook my hand.

Cynthia stopped playing the piano and came out to greet her folks.

"Merry Christmas, Cynthia," Phyllis and Ted said together.

"A very Merry Christmas to you and you," Cynthia replied.

Making a show of sniffing the air, Ted asked, "Is that Christmas Ambrosia Cheesecake I smell baking in the oven?"

That made Cynthia smile. "Indeed, it is, father of mine. I came over early and woke these two up so I could have it ready in time."

"She did actually wake us up," Maeve said. "She was here bright and early."

Stepping up to the role of host, I asked, "Would anyone like some coffee? I was just getting ready to start a pot. I'm afraid it won't be as good as what Maeve and I had at my folks this morning."

"Why is that?" Phyllis asked.

"Owen's grinding his own coffee these days," Maeve said. "He's come up with a special blend that is something else."

"The best I can offer is Maxwell House," I said. "I hope that's okay with everyone."

"That'll work for me," Ted said.

"I'm fine with that," Cynthia and Phyllis said together.

"Mom and Dad, why don't you go in and get comfortable by the fire?" Maeve said. "I'll help Mike with the coffee."

"Actually, dear," Phyllis said, "I need your husband and your father to get some gifts and groceries out of the car for me. Cynthia's gotten her part of dinner started. I guess I should too. The ham will need to roast for a good while."

"In that case, Mike, you go help Dad, and I'll make the coffee," Maeve said.

"Yes, ma'am," Ted and I said together before heading out to the car.

By noon everyone had arrived, and there was a pile of presents under the tree and a pile of food in the kitchen. We ate, exchanged gifts, ate dessert, exchanged stories, ate a little more, and then they all went home. Maeve and I collapsed on the couch in front of the dying embers in the fireplace, cups of eggnog in our hands, satisfied all had gone well.

Raising my cup in a toast to the day, I said, "Merry Christmas, baby."

She clinked her glass against mine and said, "Merry Christmas, Mike."

CHAPTER THIRTY

January 1984

After New Year's Day, at Maeve's insistence, I took Derrick up on his offer to spend a few days of Winter Break with him in Nags Head. Maeve couldn't go because she'd just started student teaching at Laney High School. I flew up in the Cessna.

There was a light crosswind from west to east as I made my final approach to the airport at Manteo. Derrick met me at the general aviation terminal. He had someone with him, and some news.

"Mike, I'd like you to meet Vanessa Hernandez. Vanessa, this is my friend and ex-roommate, Mike Lanier."

Vanessa held out her hand. "My pleasure, Mike. Derrick has told me quite a lot about you."

"The pleasure's all mine," I said, taking her hand. "I can only imagine what Derrick's told you."

Vanessa was a pleasure to meet. She was beautiful

- dusky skin, jet black hair past her shoulders, and sparkling brown eyes that invited a smile.

"Vanessa's a sophomore at State," Derrick told me as we got into his car. He and Vanessa sat up front. "Her family just moved to Kill Devil Hills from Durham. They opened this really good Mexican restaurant you've got to try. They specialize in Mexican-style seafood. We're having dinner there tonight."

"That sounds cool," I said. "I love Mexican food. But I'm not very familiar with Mexican-style seafood."

Vanessa picked up on my hesitant tone. "You're in for a treat then. We'll show you how to enjoy authentic Mexican seafood," she assured me with a smile.

Before I could ask Derrick how he wound up working in a Mexican seafood restaurant, he told me. "Mr. Hernandez had just opened the restaurant when I got home for Christmas Break. He was hiring. You can imagine jobs are few out here in winter. I jumped at the chance. That's how I met Vanessa."

The way Derrick said the part about meeting Vanessa told me a lot about how he felt about her. She showed she returned the feeling by reaching up and gently brushing her fingers along his chin.

Turning to me, she said, "Mike, I'm sorry that your wife couldn't come. I'd love to meet her."

I explained Maeve wanted to come, but she'd just started her student teaching and couldn't get away.

I'd reserved a cottage at the Sea Foam Motel, right on the ocean. It being January, I doubted I'd spend much time on the beach. After I checked in, we went for lunch at the Dunes. The food was always good there, and it was close to my hotel.

While we waited for our food, I learned more about Derrick's new girlfriend. "Vanessa, what's your major at State?"

"Business administration," Vanessa said. "My father hopes I'll eventually take over the books for the restaurant."

"Vanessa's dad was working for his brother at a restaurant in Durham before he decided to strike out on his own," Derrick added.

"He's taking a risk opening a new restaurant out here in the winter," I said.

Vanessa took a deep breath and nodded slowly before replying. "We hoped to open last summer, but things took longer than we planned. We're open now, and business has been better than we thought it'd be. I think we're attracting a lot of interest because there's no other place like it on the Outer Banks."

"It's definitely not your typical Mexican Restaurant," Derrick said. "It's one of only two or three like it in all of North Carolina."

After lunch, we took Vanessa to Kill Devil Hills and dropped her off at the restaurant. I asked Derrick what time he had to be at work.

"Vanessa's dad gave me the night off when he heard you were coming up, as long as I promised to bring you by for dinner. Vanessa has some bookkeeping things to take care of. She'll join us for dinner. I hope you don't mind, but my mom and dad,

Uncle Leon, Aunt Joan, and Paula will be coming."

"I don't mind. It'll be good to see them again."

We'd no sooner started back down the highway towards Nag's Head when a police car pulled up behind us and flashed the blue lights.

"Hey, that's Paula," Derrick said. He slowed down and started to pull over, but she pulled up beside us, waved, honked, and hurried off down the road.

"She had a busy New Year's Eve. A bunch of tourists got drunk and tried to climb the Wright Brothers Memorial to fire off bottle rockets. They managed to get lost wandering around the grounds in the dark. The cops rounded up the last of them around dawn on New Year's Day. The poor guy was half frozen."

Derrick snorted a laugh and shook his head. "He made a full recovery. I guess he had enough 80-proof anti-freeze in him."

We made it to Derrick's house with no further incidents. His mom came out of the kitchen as we walked in. "Hello, Michael. It's good to see you."

Mrs. Carson held her arms out, and I obliged her with a hug. "It's good to see you, too, Mrs. Carson. How've you been? Did you have a nice Christmas?"

"It was very nice, Michael, thank you. And how 'bout you?"

"Yes, ma'am, we had both of our families over to the new house."

"That sounds like quite a time," Mrs. Carson said. "I've got some shopping needs doing. I'll leave you boys to catch up on things."

After grabbing a couple of sodas from the fridge, Derrick and I took seats in the living room.

"Vanessa seems like a really nice girl," I said, hinting for him to tell me more about her.

Derrick flopped back in his chair and smiled. "She's great. We hit it off right away. She helped me learn my way around the restaurant, and I helped her learn her way around the island."

He leaned forward and set his drink on the coffee table, careful to use a coaster. "Wait until you try Del Mar tonight. You'll be impressed. I've been eating seafood all my life, and I've never tasted anything like it. Everyone I know who's tried it loves it."

"I can hardly wait," I said. Trying to steer the conversation back to his new girlfriend, I asked, "Where are things with you and Vanessa?"

Derrick's brow furrowed. He bit his bottom lip and nodded his head. "It's kind of hard to say. I mean, I like her, and I think she likes me. She asked to come today when I told her I was picking you up at the airport. We talk at work and take our meal breaks together. But we haven't had a chance to go on an actual date. Lunch with you today was the first time we've had a meal together outside Del Mar."

"Does her dad know you two have a thing for each other?"

Derrick shrugged but said, "Probably, but he hasn't said anything one way or the other."

I went to set my empty soda can down on the coffee table. Derrick absently pushed a coaster my way. "What about your folks? Have they said anything?"

"No," Derrick said. "I've mentioned Vanessa a few times, so they may have an inkling that I like her."

"Is Vanessa gonna eat with us tonight?"

Derrick shrugged again. "I asked her to. She said she'll have to check with her father. I'll just have to wait and see."

I thought back to something Rhiannon told me a long time ago about when a girl says she has to check with her parents. *"I'd really like to, but I'll have to ask my parents means she really wants to but isn't sure her parents will let her."*

A pained smile curled my lips at the memory. Derrick was watching me, clearly wondering what I was thinking. I sat up straight and asked, "What time are we supposed to eat dinner?"

Derrick blinked slowly and lowered his chin. I could tell from the look on his face that he knew that wasn't what I'd been thinking about. "What, are you hungry already?"

"No, I'm just wondering what we're doing between now and then," I said.

Derrick rose from his chair and said, "We, my friend, are going to Manteo. There's something at the aquarium I want to show you."

Puzzled, I followed Derrick to his car. We made our way to Roanoke Island and the North Carolina Aquarium there. The Aquarium is one of three along the North Carolina coast, the other two being at Pine Knoll Shores, near Morehead City, and Fort Fisher, south of Wilmington.

We arrived at the aquarium and approached the ticket counter. Derrick took out his wallet and removed his student ID. "We get the student discount if we show our IDs."

"I can go you one better," I said, taking out my wallet. "We have a family membership. I can get us in free."

Stuffing his wallet back in his pocket, Derrick said, "Free beats a discount every time."

My membership card didn't actually show a family membership. It showed an extremely rare, paid-up-for-life, Founders' membership. We did get in for free. What I hadn't expected was the director coming out to greet us personally.

"Mr. Lanier, I'd like to welcome you and your guest to the aquarium today. Is this your first visit to our facility?"

"It's been a while since I was here," I said. "Several years."

"I've been every year since you opened," Derrick said. "But I live in Nags Head. Mike's from Wrightsville Beach."

The director rubbed his chin and nodded. "I see. Then you must be familiar with our aquarium at Fort Fisher. I think you'll be pleased to see the additions and improvements we've made here since your last visit. If you have any questions, my staff is at your service."

I took his offered hand and said, "Thank you, sir. I'm sure we'll enjoy ourselves."

"Enjoy your visit," the director said, shaking

Derrick's hand. With a last nod at me, he turned and hastened back to his office.

Derrick, eyes narrowed, lips twisted into a half-smile, half-frown, was looking at me, obviously waiting for an explanation.

"What?" I asked.

Derrick chuckled and said, "Mike, I'm sure the director of the aquarium does not come out and greet every family membership holder who comes in the door."

"It's a slow day," I said. "Maybe he was bored sitting around his office."

"Yeah, okay. You stick to that story, okay. C'mon, I want to show you something."

He headed into the aquarium, but instead of going to the exhibits, he turned and headed to the gift shop, and then past the gift shop. I mentally kicked myself when I realized where he was going.

Derrick stopped in front of the large bronze plaque listing major donors to the aquarium. He was pointing to one listing under the Founders heading.

"Check this out, Mike. That is you, right?"

He was pointing to a line that read, "Lanier Marine Science Foundation."

I gave him a sheepish grin. "Guilty."

"Guilty? Dude, that's so cool," Derrick said. "I mean, I knew you had money, but getting on that list takes lots of money."

My brow furrowed. I bit my lip and closed my eyes for a second. When I opened them again, I quietly asked Derrick if he'd told anyone about it.

He seemed surprised at my reaction. "What? No! I mean ... why not?"

"Derrick, that membership card I showed to get in - there aren't many like it. Only those names up there have them."

"Okay. But why don't you want anyone to know?" Derrick asked. "I mean, couldn't you have kept the name off there?"

"It's complicated, but no, you can't donate that kind of money for a project like this and remain anonymous. How did you know for sure it was me?"

Derrick would not be distracted. "First, what is the big deal about people knowing?"

I gestured out the door toward the picnic area. "Let's grab a soda, and I'll try to explain."

We went through the gift shop to the snack bar. Derrick got us a couple of sodas, and we took a seat by the window.

"You've always known I had plenty of money, right?" I asked.

Derrick set his soda down and raised his eyebrows. "Uh, the classic car, the planes, the boats, the house on the river - those were all pretty good clues. Remember, my family is full of cops."

"Okay, you know all that. But when we first became roommates, you didn't know all that. You just knew I was Mike Lanier, a Navy vet, a college freshman. A couple of years older, but just a regular guy."

"Well, maybe not a regular guy," Derrick joked. "But yeah, when we first met, I had no idea you were rich."

I continued. "We became friends, and over time you figured it out. I never lied about it, but I never boasted about it or tried to be flashy about it, right?"

"The GTO was a little flashy, but no, you never tried to hide that money wasn't a problem for you. But you never made a show of how much you had, either."

"Maeve told me once that you and Hans were friends I could count on because you became my friends despite my having money, not because of it. Outside of a select few I served with in the Navy, you two are among the few guys I count among my real friends."

Derrick digested what I said. "I think I understand. You keep the money thing as low key as you can. That way you know people like you and not your money."

"That's about the size of it," I said.

Derrick punched me on the shoulder and laughed. "Well, now that I know, don't think you can start putting on airs with me. You'll always be just plain old, not quite regular, Mike."

"Thanks, man," I said. "Now, do we have time to check this place out, or do we need to head back across the water?"

"We have time for a quick walk around," Derrick said. "Then we'll head back and get ready."

We took a quick tour of the aquarium, trying to notice what was new. Most of it seemed new to me since I hadn't been there in so long. I wondered if the director would show up when we were leaving. He didn't.

I bought some trinkets for Maeve in the gift shop, and then we headed back to my hotel. Derrick told me he'd be back in an hour to pick me up and we'd go straight to Del Mar. I changed into some nicer clothes Maeve insisted I bring along, just in case. With nothing to do but wait for Derrick, I sat down and called Maeve.

"That sounds like some talk you two had," Maeve said. "Did you know your name was on that plaque?"

"I guess I knew the Foundation was listed as a contributor, but I never imagined anyone would connect it with me. I was only fifteen at the time."

"At least Derrick understands why you want to keep it low key," Maeve said.

"Yeah, you were right about him. To Derrick, I'm just his buddy Mike, who happens to have money. But so what? I'm not such a bad guy."

"You're tolerable enough when you're not being maudlin. What's this place he's taking you for dinner tonight?"

I smiled at the phone. "Maudlin, are you sure that's the right word?"

She just laughed.

"To answer your other question, it's a Mexican seafood place called Del Mar. He's sort of seeing the owner's daughter, Vanessa. She's quite pretty. She's a sophomore at State."

"What do you mean 'he's sort of seeing' her?" Maeve asked. "Are they dating?"

"They see each other at work every day, but they haven't had a chance to actually go out on a date.

Today when they picked me up and took me to lunch was the first time they'd been outside the restaurant together," I said. Changing the subject, I asked, "So how was school today?"

"The kids were pretty good. I have a ton of work, though," Maeve said. "Reflecting on today's lesson, revising my plans for tomorrow. What time is Derrick picking you up?"

Before I could answer, I heard a car pull up in front of the cottage. "I think that's him now. I'll call you later. I love you."

"I Love You. Talk to you later," Maeve said.

CHAPTER THIRTY-ONE

January 1984

Derrick knocked seconds later. We made our way back up the island to the Del Mar Restaurante. Vanessa's father, Senor Hernandez, greeted us warmly and led us to a table where Derrick's parents and his sister Linda were already seated. Derrick's Uncle Leon and his wife were with them. Paula hadn't arrived yet. Leon told us she'd be along shortly.

Senor Hernandez raised his hand and waved for a server to take our drink order. He graced Derrick with a tight smile and told him that Vanessa would join us directly. She had one or two things to finish up in the back.

The server, Maria, was taking our drink orders when Paula arrived. I was stunned. Paula was wearing a black knee-length skirt and dark gray blouse. With her short hair, there was nothing to hide the diamond earrings that adorned her ears, and she wore a shimmering diamond choker. It was the first time I'd seen Paula in anything but a police uniform, but that's not what stunned me.

Paula walked in on the arm of a man attired in the prescribed uniform of a United States Navy Lieutenant Commander. Upon his breast pocket was the insignia of a Navy Special Boat Squadron. I stared in disbelief at Lieutenant, now Lieutenant Commander, Richard Hoffman. He pulled up short when he saw me, too.

"Mike, is that you?" Richard asked. He sounded as surprised as I felt.

With Pavlovian reflexes, I rose out of my seat and came to attention. "Yes, sir, it's me," I said. Then I relaxed a little. "How are you, Rick?"

Paying no attention to anyone else in the room, Rick and I closed the distance between us and embraced. I knew I'd have to explain how Rick and I knew each other, but right then I didn't care. I was just so glad to see him.

Rick stepped back and looked me over, like he was inspecting me.

"Paula told me we'd be having dinner with a friend of the family who'd been in the Navy. Mike, I never could have dreamed it'd be you."

"I had no idea you'd be coming, sir. It's really good to see you," I said.

We realized everyone was staring at us. An explanation was in order. Rick took it upon himself to offer one.

"Mike and I served together in the Navy." Rick chuckled. "You've probably figured that out. I was his skipper for a while."

Paula, still standing, gave us an odd look. "We sort of figured it had to be something like that. Small world. Why don't we sit down, and you can tell us all about it?"

I reclaimed my seat. Paula introduced Rick to the others at our table. They ordered drinks from the patient young Maria, and Rick began the story of how we knew each other.

"Mike - back then he was Petty Officer Lanier - and I served together in what most civilians think of as the Brown-Water Navy. During Vietnam it was called Riverine forces. Anyway, we were on a training mission down in Central America. We were making our way up some river whose name I don't even recall ..."

I thought to myself, *he recalls it alright*. Rick surprised me by even talking about it. It was one of President Reagan's black ops. To my knowledge, it was still classified.

"...when we ran into some gentlemen who were up to something they didn't want us privy to, running arms bought with drug money to the rebels. They proceeded to let us know quite strenuously how unhappy they were we'd discovered their route."

As Rick spoke, I could almost smell the jungle again, feel the heat, see the brown water of the river being pierced by the bow of our boat.

We came around a bend in the river that was supposed to be a mile or so from the crossing point being used by these gentlemen. Instead, it was the crossing point, and it was in use at the time. We were hit from both sides. Rick went down right away. Tom and Snickers - we called him that because he always had a Snickers bar in his pocket - each opened fire.

I fire-walled the throttles and spun the wheel hard to port. The boat practically turned on its axis. Kevin opened fire with the rear guns on the north shore while Tom kept the south shore hot with his guns. Snickers had gone down when an RPG exploded against his turret. Shrapnel from that caught me in the hip and leg, but I hung on to the wheel.

I got the boat straightened out and sped downriver away from the ambush. Kevin maintained his fire until we were clear of the site. I kept us moving downriver towards our base while Kevin performed triage on the others.

Rick looked up at me and said, "Guess the boys with the briefcases got that one wrong," just before passing out. I radioed ahead that we were coming in with casualties. Tom caught some shrapnel but could help Kevin with the others. Snickers wasn't moving. Kevin said he didn't look too good.

Snickers didn't make it back to base camp. Rick was hit pretty badly. Kevin patched him up as best he could. I brought the boat in hot and jammed it into reverse just in time to stop us from slamming against the pilings. When I let go of the wheel, the world seemed to spin, and I dropped to the deck.

"My God, Tom, Mike's hit bad!" I heard Kevin say.

That was the last thing I heard for a while. The medics put Rick and me onto a chopper and flew us out of there. Tom had his cuts and scrapes patched up while Kevin saw to the boat. She had so many holes in her, it was a wonder she hadn't sunk on the way back.

Considering what we ran into, it was a wonder any of us made it back. That was the last time anyone was sent out on single-boat patrols. A few months later, the program was shut down, and they all went home.

Rick and I were transported to the States and wound up at Bethesda. Rick had taken rounds in the gut, but they managed to patch him up. His recuperation lasted for months.

Mine lasted over a year. My left hip was shattered, as was most of my left shin, along with miscellaneous other wounds. The hip they replaced. The shin was put back together with plates and screws. I lost a lot of blood, and it'd been touch-and-go for a while.

When Tom came to see me after Snickers' memorial service, he told me they couldn't believe I brought the boat in hit like I was. Once Rick could get up and around, he stopped by to see me nearly every day until they sent him home on convalescent leave. I hadn't seen him since he'd left Bethesda.

Maria's voice saying she'd brought my drink brought my attention back to the present. I heard Rick saying, "...to make a long story short, Mike's quick reaction to the situation probably saved our lives."

They all looked at me, but I looked at Rick. I didn't say anything. He could tell I was thinking I wasn't quick enough to save Snickers.

"It was a terrible day, that's for sure," I said. "Rick, are you still with the boats?"

Rick finished his drink and said, "No, I'm in the black shoe Navy now. XO on a Perry Class out of Norfolk. I heard the Navy medically discharged you after your rehab."

I nodded slowly. "They did. I'm in college now and married."

"No kidding. Congratulations," Rick said, looking around as if expecting to see my wife close by. "Will she be here tonight?"

"Mike's on his own this trip," Paula answered before I could say anything.

"Maeve's a student teacher," Derrick added. "She can't just up and fly off any time like old Mike here."

Hoping to change the subject, I said, "Enough about old Mike, I think. Paula, how did you wind up meeting my old skipper?"

Paula chuckled and cast a sideways glance at Rick. "I wrote him a speeding ticket."

"It's the truth," Rick said, shrugging and shaking his head. "When she found out I was a sailor rushing to get back to my ship, she took pity on me and gave me a warning."

"When he got back from Grenada, he called and asked me to dinner," Paula said, finishing the story. "We've been seeing each other whenever the Navy gives him a chance to come down here ever since."

"Yes," Leon said with a knowing smile. "They've become quite a pair. You wouldn't think a Naval

Officer would find much to like about an old Army MP, would you?"

Saving us from any further Army-Navy rivalry, Maria returned to take our food order and deliver fresh drinks. Vanessa joined us when the drinks arrived and sat next to Derrick. Conversation turned to more mundane things. Before long, the food arrived.

As Derrick promised, it was something special. I may have had better seafood, but I don't remember where or when.

When the party broke up, Rick took me aside. "Mike, it was good to see you. I hope we can do this again soon."

"Rick, if you're in port in late June, come on down to Wilmington with Paula. I'm throwing a big party - formal affair - so bring your whites."

"If I can make it, I'll be there."

After a handshake that became a brotherly hug, Rick hurried off to join Paula. I said good night to Leon and his wife and looked around for Derrick.

"He's still inside with Vanessa," his father told me. "Mrs. Carson and I need to be going, Mike. We hope you enjoyed dinner."

"Yes, sir, thank you, I did."

Mrs. Carson gave me a hug. "We always knew you were a special fellow, Michael. I guess we shouldn't be surprised to learn you're also a hero."

In a soft voice I said, "I'm no hero, Mrs. Carson. I just did what I needed to do."

She patted my arm. "Well, I'll go on thinking you're

a hero. You and Derrick have a good time now. Don't stay out too late."

"Leave the boy alone, mother. They'll be fine," Mr. Carson said, holding out his hand to shake mine. "Good night, Mike."

"Good night, sir, ma'am," I said.

Standing alone in the parking lot, I started wondering where Derrick was when he came walking out with Vanessa.

Derrick looked to be in a particularly good mood. "Okay, where to now, Mikey?"

That struck a nerve. "Don't ever call me Mikey. And I don't know where to. This is your town."

I shouldn't have snapped at him that way. Derrick didn't know not to call me that.

"Sorry, Mike, just caught up in the moment. You're right. This is my town. I know just where we should go."

He did know just where to go. We had a great time. Though I think he may have enjoyed himself more if I'd just gone back to the hotel, Derrick insisted not. But he dropped me off before taking Vanessa home.

It was late, but I'd promised Maeve I'd call no matter how late I got in.

"Hello, Mike, is that you?" Maeve asked, stifling a yawn. Judging from how long it took her to answer the phone, I must have roused her from a sound sleep.

"Yes, sweetheart, it's me. I just got in. Derrick was showing me the town."

"Did you have a good time?" Maeve asked, followed by a loud yawn she couldn't suppress.

Smiling to myself, I replied, "Yes, dear, I did, or at least I tried to."

"That's good, honey. You can tell me all about it when you get home."

Knowing she had to be at school early, I decided not to keep her on the phone.

"Okay. Goodnight. I love you."

"I uv u to," Maeve said as she hung up the phone.

I got ready for bed but couldn't fall asleep right away. Seeing Rick got me thinking about things. I replayed that fateful day in my head again, asking myself what we could have done differently.

The answer kept coming back - nothing. We followed the mission parameters. When we got hit, we returned fire and shot our way out of the ambush. The after action said we'd done as well as anyone could have, and better than most.

Though it was by accident, we'd discovered a previously unknown conduit the bad guys were using, which was ultimately shut down. In a sealed section of all our service records, there were secret commendations testifying to the great job we'd done. The official story was that we'd hit a mine left behind in some previous banana republic civil war. *Yeah*, I thought as I drifted off to sleep; *everyone knows how mines can make so many bullet holes.*

CHAPTER THIRTY-TWO

January 1984

After our late night, it felt like my head had just hit the pillow when Derrick came to the door ready and raring to go.

"How in the world can you be this energized at this hour of the morning after last night?" I asked.

"Clean living," Derrick chided me. "Let's get going. Time for some fishing."

Yawning and stretching, I asked, "Is it even above freezing out there?"

"Are you kidding?" Derrick replied, much too cheerfully. "It's already over forty with the high predicted near sixty. Let's hit the water."

It rarely takes much persuasion to get me out on the water, but I was having a hard time getting my motor running. "Are we at least stopping for breakfast along the way?"

"You better believe it," Derrick said. He looked at his watch and tapped the crystal. "Or at the rate you're going, maybe lunch."

"All right, all right, I'm coming," I said.

We stopped for breakfast at a place that had quotes and anecdotes painted on the rafters and ceiling molding. The ceiling beams were painted in a random mix of bright oranges, yellows, reds, and greens. Derrick and I ate our fill before heading down to the marina in Wanchese, on the south end of the island.

"My dad said we could use his boat. Mine's too small for such an excursion as this." Derrick pointed to a twelve-foot aluminum boat resting upside down on the sand near the dock.

"What kind of boat does your dad have?" I remembered Mr. Carson talking about buying a boat during dinner but couldn't recall the details.

"I'll let him tell you," Derrick said.

I looked down the dock and saw John and Leon Carson waiting for us, standing next to a very nice Grady-White boat.

"Well, Mike, what do you think? Not too bad, eh?" John asked.

Looking at the boat, I was impressed. "Not bad at all, Mr. Carson. She looks brand new."

John's smile made me think of a proud father. "Leon and I haven't had her long. We picked her up at the end of July, just as the new models were coming out. We got quite a deal on her."

"She's a Grady-White Trophy Pro 25," Leon said. "With a pair of 150 horse Johnsons on back. She'll get us there and back at warp speed. We got all the bells and whistles."

Derrick motioned for me to board and followed me onto the boat. "Okay then, let's get her out on the sound. We've already spent half the day talking."

"Patience, nephew," Leon said. "We've got to give Michael the nickel tour."

"I'll show Michael the boat," John said. "Leon, you and Derrick get us underway."

"Now you're talking, Dad, let's go."

While John gave me a quick tour of the boat, Derrick and Leon took us out onto the sound. They decided we'd fish the sound instead of heading offshore. The forecast was for strengthening winds out on the ocean, and none of us felt much like fighting our way home through that. There was enough room in the sound to let them show me what the boat could do. It was even more impressive out on the water.

After a little cruising to show off the boat's speed and power, we tried several spots where the fish were reported to be biting despite the winter weather. We had a little luck, but the wind picked up, and we soon found ourselves anchored near the boat landing, gathered in the cozy little cabin, nursing cups of coffee from a thermos thoughtfully provided by Derrick's mom.

I took a cautious sip and said, "You've got quite a nice fishing boat here, gentlemen."

"Thank you, Mike," John said, tipping his cup to me.

Leon set his cup down. His eyes narrowed, and his lips formed a thin line as he studied my face. He turned to John, who nodded, and then he turned to me.

"Now that we've got you out here, Mike, away from the ladies, we'd like to ask you something."

I couldn't imagine what. "Yes, sir."

Looking me right in the eye, John asked, "That tale Rick told last night, how much was fact, and how much was a smokescreen?"

"I'm really not supposed to talk about that," I said. "I was surprised Rick said as much as he did."

Derrick looked from his uncle to his father and finally at me. "If you can't tell us, Mike, we understand."

I took a deep breath and another sip of coffee. "Oh, I'll tell you. If I can't trust you three, who can I trust? But you must understand this can go no further. This is one of those 'I'll tell you, but then I have to kill you' things."

Leon shared a look with John, who gave a just-perceptible nod. They turned to Derrick. Derrick pursed his lips and nodded, too.

Leon turned to me and said, "We understand, Mike."

Taking another sip of my coffee gave me time to gather my thoughts. "The official story is that we were on a training mission in Panama when the boat hit a mine leftover from who knows when."

I related the whole unvarnished truth to them. It felt good to tell someone at last. When I was done, no one said anything for several minutes.

Derrick finally broke the silence. "Whoa, Mike, I had no idea."

John shook his head and shrugged. "I guess things like that happen more often than we'd like to think."

"Yeah, I guess they do," I said.

Leon topped off our cups with the last of the coffee. We sat quietly until John suggested it was time to head in. We motored back to the landing and got the boat onto the trailer. John and Leon left for home. Derrick and I headed to my hotel.

"Mike, I just want you to know, all that hero stuff ... I'll still expect you to salute me after I get my commission."

Leave it to Derrick to put it all in perspective.

"If you're gonna wait for a salute from me, you're going to be waiting a very long time," I said.

We both started laughing.

CHAPTER THIRTY-THREE

January 1984

I flew back to Wilmington a couple of days later. Visiting Derrick and his family was fun, but I was eager to get back to Maeve.

Friday morning, I dropped Maeve at Laney High before visiting the airport and checking on the Cessna. We'd be flying to River Dream for the weekend. It was the last weekend before my spring semester started, and we wanted to make the most of it.

Having made sure the Cessna was loaded and ready, I met Maeve for lunch in the school cafeteria. That brought back memories.

"Are you thinking about the last time you were here?" Maeve asked after we took our seats.

My lips curved up in a wistful smile. "It seems like

a lifetime ago. Let's see if I can remember."

I sat up straight and turned my head to get a good look around. "Our table was over there by the windows."

Maeve looked at the group of kids eating there. "Who would have been sitting there?"

"Most days, me and Rhiannon, Hans and April, Jill, Wesley, Beth and what was Wesley's girlfriend's name?"

"There were so many you can't remember them all?" Maeve asked. I could tell by her grin that she was teasing.

I furrowed my brow and tried hard to remember. "Allyson, her name was Allyson. She was so mad when Wesley shipped out for boot camp and missed graduation."

"I know about Rhiannon and Jill," Maeve said with mock sternness. "Who was Beth?"

"Beth Bosworth," I said. "She used to hang out with us at lunch."

"Is that all?" Maeve asked. Her tone said she thought there was more to it than that.

"She was one of my best friends once upon a time," I said sadly. "I haven't seen her in ages."

"I knew there was more to the story," Maeve said. "She student taught here last spring with my lead teacher. She's at that private school, SENCLand Academy, now. I guess they offered her a good deal."

"They probably did. They have a goal of paying state scale plus ten percent, you know."

Maeve picked up her napkin and cleaned a bit of

ketchup from her chin. "No, I didn't know that. How do you know?"

"When they were starting, the trust gave them a decent endowment. I get, or I should say, my dad gets regular financial reports. I think my mom sits on their board."

Maeve's face scrunched into a frown. "And you never mentioned this because ...?"

"Sweetheart, the trust has put so much into different things all over coastal Carolina, I rarely think about it unless something specifically gets mentioned."

"I don't think I'd want to work there anyway. Isn't it mostly for rich kids?" Maeve asked.

"That's a common misconception. What's wrong with rich kids, anyway?" I asked with mock indignation. "I was a rich kid."

"You, my darling, are the exception to the rule," Maeve assured me. "You always went to public schools."

"Hm," I replied, unconvinced. "Just the same, twenty-five percent of the academy's students come from disadvantaged neighborhoods. As the endowment grows, so does the percentage. That was a condition of the gift from the trust."

"I didn't know that," Maeve said. "Still, I like it here at Laney."

We ate in silence for a few minutes, and then Mrs. Porter, who was Miss Royalle when I went to school there, giggled.

"Mrs. Lanier, I think you and your husband have

become the topic of conversation at that table over there." She pointed to a table near the door.

Maeve and I looked to where Mrs. Porter was pointing. A group of girls were looking at us and talking animatedly among themselves. One girl seemed familiar to me, but I wasn't sure why. At the prodding of the other girls, she got up and walked over.

"Mrs. Lanier, excuse me, is this your husband?" the girl asked.

Giving the nervous girl a friendly smile, Maeve said, "Yes, Mandy, this is Mr. Lanier."

Turning to me, the young lady asked, "Is your first name Michael?"

The feeling that I should know her was growing, but it just wouldn't come to me.

"Yes, it is," I said. "And you would be?"

"I'm Mandy Hunter. You went to school with my big brother Wesley."

It all came flooding back as soon as she mentioned Wesley. He joined the Marines and left for Paris Island just days before I left for Navy training in Orlando. I hadn't seen him since.

"My goodness, Mandy, the last time I saw you, you were what - ten or eleven?" I said. "You've grown up some."

She smiled, and a faint blush colored her cheeks. "That's how old I was when Wes graduated."

"How's he doing these days?" The answer was not what I expected.

"He's getting better all the time," Mandy said.

Wondering what she meant, I asked, "Has he been sick?"

Mandy shook her head. With a hitch in her voice, she said, "No, he got hurt. He was in the Marine barracks in Lebanon when it got blown up. For a while, he couldn't walk. Now he gets around pretty well with his cane."

For a moment, I couldn't find my voice. The news hit me hard. "I didn't know he was there."

"Yeah," said Mandy, "he was lucky. He should be good as new once everything heals, and he does his physical therapy. He'll even be able to stay in the Corps."

He was one up on me there. The Navy hadn't wanted to keep me.

"Is that what he wants to do?"

Mandy shrugged. "I don't know. Some days he says he wants to. Sometimes he says he can't wait until his enlistment is up. He just re-enlisted last May."

I saw her friends finishing their lunches and getting ready to leave. "Tell him Mike says hi. I hope he gets well soon."

"Okay, I sure will. See ya." Mandy turned and hurried back to her friends.

Something about the look on my face must have worried Maeve. "Honey, are you okay? That was some tough news."

I closed my eyes and gathered my thoughts before answering. "I had no idea that Wes was in Lebanon, much less that he was wounded."

"It's scary," Maeve said. "At least nothing like that

happened to you."

"Yeah," was all I said, barely loud enough for her to hear.

The bell rang, and Maeve had to go back to class to finish out the day.

I headed out to the football field, where I sat in the bleachers and waited for her. It wasn't a cold day, but the PE classes were all in the gym. I had the place to myself.

I thought a lot about what happened to Wesley, about running into Rick again, and about what I needed to tell Maeve about what I'd actually done in the Navy. I'd given her the impression that I'd driven around in small boats dropping people off on beaches like a ferry operator.

After a great deal of thinking, I decided I'd tell her when we were on the boat on our way to Morehead City. That would give us plenty of time alone to talk about it and let me answer questions she might ask. I should have known my plan wouldn't survive Maeve's curiosity.

The last bell rang. I headed back toward the building. When I walked into her classroom, Maeve closed the door and asked me to sit down.

"Michael, I can't shake the feeling there's something you need to tell me, but maybe you haven't been able to find the right words, the right time, or whatever. Now would be a good time before we go home for the weekend."

I settled into a student desk. "Maeve, I don't know if this is the time or place."

Maeve sat in the desk next to me. "It'll have to do, because we're sitting here until we've talked about this."

"Are you sure you wouldn't rather wait until we get to River Dream?"

She shook her head slowly. "I'm sure, Michael. Ever since you got back from visiting Derrick, I've sensed something's bothering you. After you found out about Wesley, my intuition went into overdrive. I'm worried, Michael. If something is bothering you, I want to help you with it."

Meeting her gaze and seeing the concern in her eyes, I said, "I don't know if there's anything you can do to help."

She sat up straight. "I knew there was something."

Then she leaned toward me and took my hands in hers. "I love you, Michael. Whatever's troubling you isn't yours alone. It's ours now. Whatever it is, we can face it together."

"I love you too, Maeve. I love you so much," I said, around the lump forming in my throat. Pulling myself together, I decided the time had come.

"Today at lunch, after Mandy came over and told us about Wesley, you said that at least nothing like that had happened to me. What I'm about to tell you is still classified. This is what happened."

I told her all of it. I told her about the clandestine river patrols we'd run. I told her about the firefights we'd gotten into. I told her about that day when Snickers got killed, and how I blamed myself for not being fast enough to get us out of there.

I told her how Rick was nearly killed, how I'd been wounded, and how Kevin was the only one who came out of it without a scratch, only to be killed by a drunk driver after we returned home. I told her Rick and I were airlifted out.

I told her about all the surgeries and the months of therapy. I told her about the secret commendations in my file. I told her almost all of it. I didn't tell her how I'd waited and waited in vain for Rhiannon to come. Through it all, she never said a word. Finally, I wound down.

"Until I saw Rick the other night, I'd tried not to think too much about it. It wasn't a glorious time. We weren't supposed to talk about it. The government wanted it to be like it never happened. I tried to put it out of my mind. I'm sorry."

Her voice just above a whisper, Maeve asked, "Why are you sorry?"

"I'm sorry I didn't tell you before. That I didn't tell you all of it."

She reached up and gently placed her hand on my cheek. "Sweetheart, you have nothing to be sorry for. I knew you were in the Navy, but I never really asked you what you did there. I saw your scars and never pressed you about how you got them. If anyone should be sorry, it's me. I could have asked. I didn't have to let you carry this alone."

"Maeve, please, baby, you've helped me more than you know. I never realized how much I'd bottled it up inside until I saw Rick the other night. Then, when I heard about Wes today, I realized I had to share this with you, tell you the whole story. I needed you to know."

"Now I know. Now that elephant is no longer in the room with us. Now, Michael, take me home to River Dream," Maeve said, rising and pulling me up with her.

As I took Maeve in my arms, I offered a silent prayer of thanks to God for sending this woman to me. I hadn't realized until that very afternoon, in that classroom, just how much I'd needed her to re-enter my life right when she did. I hated to imagine what might have happened to me if she hadn't.

We left the school, drove to the airport, and flew home to River Dream.

About the Author

My writing reflects my memories growing up along the North Carolina coast near Wrightsville and Carolina Beaches. I left that area when I graduated high school and traveled half-way around the world and back, collecting memories and experiences which help shape my characters. Now back in eastern North Carolina, I enjoy bringing to life characters whose adventures take place in my favorite part of the world.

ACKNOWLEDGEMENT

Foremost, I want to acknowledge my most constant source of inspiration and encouragement, my lovely wife Karen. Karen, and our sons Alex and Zack, have been my cheerleaders, proofreaders, sounding boards, harshest critics, and biggest fans. I can never thank them enough.

To my editor and dear friend, Jeanie Sherman, whose support and advice have been so critical in producing a work I can be proud to offer to my readers.

To all the fans of *River Dream*, who have encouraged and cajoled me to get *Dreams Change* finished and published. You helped me see this through and go the extra mile to make it a better book than it otherwise might have been.

Thank you all so much for helping me keep my writing dream alive.

ABOUT THE AUTHOR

Dw Davis

DW's writing reflects his memories growing up along the North Carolina coast near Wrightsville and Carolina Beaches. He left that area when he graduated high school and traveled half-way around the world and back, collecting memories and experiences which  help shape his characters. Now back in eastern North Carolina, DW enjoys bringing to life characters whose adventures take place in his favorite part of the world.

THE RIVER DREAM TRILOGY

River Dream

Michael and Rhiannon, best friends as long as they can remember, are about to enter high school and face the challenges that come with it. The biggest challenge their friendship faces is their changing feelings for each other.

Michael's feelings for Rhiannon have grown beyond friendship, but she's made rules against dating her best friend.

Is it that Rhiannon doesn't feel the same about Michael, or does she fear what will happen if a romance between them doesn't work out?

As high school begins, Jill, the new girl in town, sets her sights on Michael. Will the possibility of losing Michael forever cause Rhiannon to change her rules?

And is Jill the only one who might keep Rhiannon and

Michael apart? Could there be someone else who could replace her in Michael's heart?

Dreams Adrift: A River Dream Novel

Michael and Maeve are about to renew their vows in the big, beachside wedding Maeve always dreamed of when Rhiannon's unexpected arrival threatens to derail their plans. Will Rhiannon be able to win Mike back, or will his new love for Maeve be stronger than his old feelings for his high school sweetheart?

The fates once conspired to change Michael's dreams. Are they now conspiring to set his Dreams Adrift?

BOOKS BY THIS AUTHOR

The Buzby Beach Books

Find DW's Buzby Beach Books and his other published work here.